The Restrainers
by Lauren M. Flauding

© 2016 by Lauren M. Flauding
Blurtery Publishing

All characters and events in this book are fictitious and any resemblance to real persons, living or dead, is purely coincidental.

All rights reserved. No part of this book may be reproduced, stored in a retrieval system, or transmitted, in any form or by any means, without the prior permission in writing of the author.

Chapter 1

"Mari, jump on to the roof of the next building."

There is only a slight hesitation as I run to the edge of the roof I'm on and push off into the open air, stretching my body to cover the distance between the two rooftops: about 20 feet. I bring my legs up as I near the building, landing hard on my feet and rolling forward until I'm able to get up and start running again. I open my palm and glance at the face of the timer wrapped around my hand. I only have 3 minutes left.

The past six months of grueling drills and painful exercises is culminating in this 4 and a half minute test. If I pass, I'll officially be a Restrainer. These months have been the most physically challenging of my life, and the emotional strain has added to the unpleasantness of the experience. I haven't seen my mother or Daniel since the night I escaped the Dissenter base. I haven't seen Miles since he was dragged out of the control tower by three Restrainers, on his way to prison. I shudder as I think about what they might be doing to him in the Governor's "special facility."

Stop thinking about Miles. You have to focus.

I come to an apparatus mounted on the building with several long cables attached to it.

"Mari, rappel down the side of the building and enter through the 12th story window."

I'm careful to make the command as precise as I can. I know they're watching my every move. I grab one of the cables and ease myself over the edge of the building, sliding down the cord as I descend along the wall. The building is 20 stories and I count down until I get to the 12th. The window, as expected, is closed. I kick off of the wall and slam my feet into the glass. The window shatters and I fall into a dark room. I've got blood on my hands and face, but I can't assess my injuries. I'm running out of time.

I stumble across the room, pull open the door, and am confronted by a hallway of billowing flames. I slam the door shut, nearly choking on the smoke that has poured into the room. *Great. What now?* My uniform is flammable, and the fire barricades me from accessing the rest of the building.

My mind flits back to the numerous arguments I've had with my handler, Clint.

"What are you waiting for?" He would ask.

"I'm looking for the best strategy."

"Mari, you don't need to do anything," he would reply, throwing his hands up in exasperation. "Just tell the Amplifier your goal, and it will take care of it."

I glance around the dim room until I spot something useful. The carpet.

"Mari, find out a way to make it through the fire."

I pry up a large section of the thin carpet and wrap it around me, then open the door and dive to the ground, rolling underneath the scorching flames. I'm sweating inside my carpeted cocoon as I roll blindly across the floor, but after a few seconds I hit something solid — probably a wall. I quickly shake myself out of the remains of the burning carpet and take off down another hallway, away from the fire. The sleeve on my right arm is smoking.

I round a corner and almost run straight into a massive spike jutting out from the wall. Peering down the tall corridor, I take in the rows and rows of sharp rods shooting out and then retracting back into the walls, alternating from each side every couple seconds. Each set consists of five spikes and the rows are about a foot apart. There's a fraction of a second when the spikes are retracted on both sides where I might be able to maneuver through, but even if I somehow avoid getting impaled, waiting for the rods to recede with each step forward would take way too much time. But if I can't go through, maybe I can go over.

"Mari, climb up and run on top of the spikes to the end of the hall."

I grab on to the set of spikes in front of me, pull myself up to the highest one and begin running. The ceiling is high enough that I only have to crouch down a little bit as I run nimbly on top of the sharp instruments. When I feel them start to retract in to the wall, I leap over to the other side to catch the sets of spikes that are just shooting out. It's a little nerve-wracking to be running on these thin poles that are constantly shifting beneath me, but as long as I keep forward momentum and step lightly I don't lose my balance.

I reach the end of the spikes and nearly fall off the last one. I jump to the floor and tumble a little before I can get to my feet again and continue on to my destination. I run down several more hallways until I'm almost in the center of the building. I look at the timer in my palm again. 54 seconds. At the end of the last hallway there are three doors. I don't have enough time to pick the wrong one.

"Mari, figure out the correct door."

There's smoke seeping out from underneath the third door, and the second door is rattling, so I open the first one. At first I think I've chosen the wrong door, but then I catch a glimpse of the receptacle behind the large man preparing to attack me.

"Mari, evade your opponent and get to the receptacle."

I take a few steps into the room as the man rushes toward me. Just as he's reaching out, possibly to strangle me, I drop to the floor and he trips over me, flying out the door. I get to my feet and run to the receptacle. I've almost made it to the edge of the receptacle when two powerful hands grab my shoulders and wrench me backward. The man recovered much faster than I thought he would. I writhe to try to free myself, but his grip is secure. He drags me back a few feet then turns me and starts pushing toward a wall, apparently in an attempt to smash me against it, but it's the best maneuver I could hope for.

"Mari, run up the wall and flip over your aggressor."

The man tries to change course when he hears my command, but it's too late. Using him as leverage, I run up the wall and the momentum is enough to propel me over the man, bending his arms back at an awkward angle and forcing him to release me. I complete a back flip and land on my feet. I look at the timer in my hand. 3 seconds.

I race over to the receptacle while prying the timer off of my hand. I have fractions of a second left as I slam the timer into a small slot and collapse next to the receptacle. A metallic voice fills the room.

"Explosive contained. Testing complete."

A door opens on the opposite side of the room. I look up and see my assessors and Governor Plenaris approaching. I'm breathing hard. Too hard. I close my eyes and concentrate on steadying my breathing. I have to be stronger if I'm going to make this work.

Chapter 2

"Well, Miss Quillen, you barely passed," Governor Plenaris observes, sneering. "I suppose that's to be expected of the youngest person to attempt the course."

I should probably be offended, but I'm actually pretty ecstatic. I can't believe I passed. The Governor, my handler Clint, and two other Restrainers are dismantling the receptacle.

"Hey, good job."

I whip around to see the large man who had previously attacked me walking forward and massaging his wrist.

"Uh, thanks," I reply awkwardly. It's weird to be making small talk with the man who was just trying to strangle me.

"You did things a lot differently than the others," he comments, studying me with some interest.

I don't know how to respond. Luckily, Clint barges into our conversation.

"Yeah, Mari always insists on finding the least conventional way of completing a task," he interjects, slapping me so hard on the back that I almost fall over. "She's made my life a whole lot more difficult, that's for sure."

I force a smile. Clint means well, I know I've been a challenge for him these past six months during my training, and he's helped me a lot. He's an attractive guy, in his late 20s with sandy hair and a nice smile, but his features don't make up for the fact that he's a real big jerk.

"Quillen," he hisses, pulling me aside, "you almost gave me a heart attack. Do you know how bad this would have made me look if you hadn't passed?"

"Forgive me, Clint," I respond sarcastically, "for not considering your reputation as I was almost burned, skewered, and pounded to death."

"Don't forget blown up."

"What do you mean?"

"That timer you were wearing was a bomb. If you hadn't made it in time, you would have lost more than just your chance to be a Restrainer."

"Why didn't you tell me before?"

"Fear of death should never be an incentive for completing an assignment."

"I'd say that's the *best* incentive ... "

"Regardless, you passed, you're still alive, good for you," Clint says flatly. "But," he adds, handing me an Adhesive, "I want you to watch this so you can see all the ways you could have done better."

I take the small patch and put it in the pocket of my uniform. Clint stares at me expectantly.

"Now?" I ask.

"Yes," he says sharply. "Go find a room to watch it while we're finishing up here, and then report back to me."

I reluctantly walk out to find an empty room. What's the point? I already passed the test, is he asking me to watch this just to make feel bad? If that was his plan, it's not going to work. I'm euphoric.

These past six months have been the most demanding of my life - I've never worked so hard. Moments after I agreed to become a Restrainer that night in the control tower, Governor Plenaris sent me to the implantation wing in the hospital where I received my enhanced Amplifier as well as a transmitter, a tiny chip inserted right next to the Amplifier that allows me to use Amplification outside of the Community's boundary. It was almost the same procedure as when I got Amplified the first time. Then I was immediately shipped off to a remote location south of the Community to train. It was really lonely down there. There were only 5 other people and their handlers in the entire facility, and they wanted nothing to do with me.

Somehow, they all knew who I was and how I was allowed to become a Restrainer under special circumstances and they hated that. It didn't help that I was far younger than everyone else there. Clint would instruct me, but outside of training hours he'd ditch me to go hang out with the others. I'd use that time alone to get in extra practice and exercise. I didn't go there to make friends, but sometimes it was really depressing. I'm just glad it's over. I know it's not going to get any easier, but at least I'm finally moving forward.

I walk into an empty room and sit in a corner on the floor. It feels good to rest my body. I feel like I could fall asleep here in this corner, and I probably would if the Governor wasn't a few rooms away. I couldn't risk him hearing the things I say in my sleep. I peel the backing off of the Adhesive and apply it to my temple. Immediately I'm surrounded with images from the roof I was on several minutes ago.

I watch a succession of several people going through the course. There are slight variations between them, but it's all pretty much the same. They run across the rooftops, then use their Amplifiers to scale down the side of the building and enter through the 12th story window. They locate and activate the fire alarm to extinguish the flames. They follow an intricate pattern to run, jump, twist, and swing through the sets of spikes. They attack the large man in different ways, but he always ends up unconscious on the floor. They all insert their timers into the receptacle with at least 30 seconds to spare.

Now I know the message that Clint is indirectly trying to give me, one that's become all too familiar to me over the past few years. I stand out. I'm different. If I'm going to survive as a Restrainer, I have to blend in.

―――――――

There are three of us being inducted into the Restrainer Corps today. The ceremony is short and simple, but I can't help feeling nervous. We're assembled in the huge ballroom at the Governor's mansion. The last time I was here was when I was stealing Digestion capsules. It feels a lot different having been invited here, but I'm almost just as scared.

The room is filled with Restrainers and a handful of soldiers. I automatically look for Alia among the soldiers, then cringe as I remember for the millionth time that she was one of the few taken captive by the North. I don't even know if she's alive anymore. I was cut off from everything during my training, so I have no idea what's been happening in the Community lately.

The Governor signals that it's time for the ceremony to begin. The sea of Restrainers splits in two, leaving an aisle up the middle leading to the Governor and three podiums at the front. I walk slowly up the aisle with the other two inductees, almost like the ancient wedding films we used to watch in school. I notice quite a few nasty glares from the other Restrainers. Seems like almost everyone here is unhappy about my induction.

We reach the front and each take our places behind a podium. I glance down and see a copy of The Equality Movement and The Restrainer Oath. Clint briefed me on what would happen during the induction. The Governor is saying something, but I'm not listening. I'm feverishly reading through the words of the Oath.

A Restrainer comes forward and removes the Oath from each of the podiums. Governor Plenaris instructs the first inductee on the procedure. Then the tall man gives himself the command.

"James, recite The Restrainer Oath."

I listen carefully to the words. He finishes, and the Governor moves on to the woman next to me.

"Monique, recite The Restrainer Oath."

I'm sweating. I shouldn't be sweating. I can't let my agitation show.

"Marianna Quillen," the Governor announces. I have to refrain from twitching at the sound of his voice. "Please place your left hand on the Movement and raise your right hand to take the Oath."

I steady my hands as they move to the correct positions. I look out at the room full of Restrainers and swallow hard. After what seems like hours, I finally open my mouth.

"Mari, recite The Restrainer Oath."

The words come automatically.

"I swear, upon removal of my Amplifier, to do everything within my power to serve the Community, protect the Governor, and uphold the Equality Movement."

The first of many lies I'll utter during my time as a Restrainer.

Chapter 3

I hesitate outside of Adrian's door. We haven't spoken in almost a year, and we haven't been on good terms for even longer. Plus, he thinks I'm dead. He thinks we're all dead; that my mother, Daniel, and I were all killed when our house exploded — the explosion that my mom planned to help her and Daniel escape the suspicion of the Restrainers.

What will he do when he sees me? Will he be mad? Happy? Relieved? Shocked? I would have tried to see him sooner, but it was impossible with Restrainer training and I've only been on duty in the city for a few days. I'm in between my patrols at the Mall-cruiser station, and this is the first day I've had enough free time to try and see Adrian.

Maybe this wasn't such a good idea, I think. What would I do if my estranged sister who was supposed to be dead suddenly showed up at my door? I'd probably think I was going crazy. Or at the very least, a raw, emotional wound would suddenly be reopened. *I'll do this another time,* I think, turning to leave, but then the door opens, and I'm face to face with Adrian.

"Mari?" He exclaims. His expression is unreadable. I stare at my older brother. He still looks huge and muscular, but he seems weak somehow, like underneath all that bulk he doesn't have the strength or willpower to do anything. He has dark circles under his eyes and he looks a lot older than when I last saw him.

I'm still searching for the appropriate words to come to my mind when he surges forward and envelops me with his massive arms. I return the hug tentatively at first, then feel myself melting into his embrace, letting months of pent up stress and pain drain out of my body. Tears are streaming down my face. When I pull away, I see that Adrian is crying too. He pulls me into his apartment.

"Mari, how did you ... ? I ... I don't understand ... " he stammers, looking at me incredulously.

"I was knocked unconscious in the explosion and the Dissenters found me and took me prisoner," I say, repeating the lie that Miles told the Governor in order to protect me, the lie that has been circulating among the Restrainers.

"How did you escape?" Adrian asks.

"The night the North sent in the robots, the Dissenters got a little frantic and decided to move me to another location. Along the way, the transport was overturned by some robots, and in the chaos I was able to get away." I wince as I realize I'm getting a little too good at lying.

"What about mom and Daniel?" He ventures hopefully.

I look down at my stunted finger. I guess Adrian thinks my silence means that they're dead, which is the best I could hope for right now. I can't bring myself to lie openly to him about mom and Daniel, but I can't very well tell him that they're Dissenters either. He's my brother, but I don't know if he can be trusted.

Adrian looks at me and gives me a weak smile, then his face changes as he takes in my uniform.

"Hold on, you're a Restrainer?"

I sigh. This is always the hardest part of the story to tell people. One, because it's the only part that's true, and two, because it reminds me of Miles.

"When I escaped from the Dissenters, I came into the city and saw what had happened to everyone. I was able to get into the control tower to switch the Amplifiers back on and help the Governor get rid of the robots. In return, the Governor offered me the chance to become a Restrainer."

"I can't believe it!" Adrian exclaims. "I heard the rumors that it was a *clam* who went up there, but I would never have imagined it was you!"

"I know, pretty ironic, huh?" I say flatly.

He lets out a sound that could be a laugh.

"What's been happening here in the Community?" I ask, wanting to change the subject.

"It's getting back to normal," he replies, sitting down on his couch. "People have been rebuilding and getting back to work. Right after the attack from the North, there were hundreds of people who requested to have their Amplifiers removed, but the Governor made them wait three months. When the time came around, only a handful actually went through with it."

Of course, I think. The Governor knew the trauma of being overtaken by the robots would wear off once people got used to depending on their Amplifiers again.

"Is the Override Program still in effect?" I ask.

"Yeah, but it's only been activated a couple times since the attack."

Interesting. That's probably why most of those people felt less urgency to get rid of their Amplifiers.

Suddenly, Adrian stands up and hugs me again.

"Mari, I'm so glad you're alive," he confesses. "You can't imagine how hard it's been, I've felt so alone and so helpless."

I feel so bad for him right now that I want break down and tell him mom and Daniel are actually still alive, but there's a sound at the door. I look over and see a small package being slipped under Adrian's door.

Adrian practically throws me aside and lunges toward the package, swiping it up and tearing it open. He looks at me sheepishly once he realizes I'm staring at him. He pulls out several clear pills that look like nutrition capsules, only slightly larger.

"Do you want one?" He asks hesitantly.

"What are they? What do they do?"

"They're Euphorics. They're like Intoxication capsules, but much stronger and they don't shut off your Amplifier. They're like ... here."

He pops one of the pills in his mouth. His eyes close and he looks like he's unconscious for half a second, then his face lights up with a strange smile. "They just make you feel really, really good," he states stupidly, his eyes wide and glazed over. "They started handing them out after the attack from the North to help people get past the trauma."

"Who started handing them out?"

"I don't know, people."

"You don't know who makes them or where they come from?"

"They come from my buddy down the hall."

"Where does *he* get them?"

"Why does it matter, Mari? They're great! You could bash my knees in with a metal beam right now and I wouldn't feel a thing!"

"How long do they last?"

"About an hour. You should try one!" He offers the package to me and giggles a bit.

"Maybe another time," I respond, eyeing the pill warily.

Adrian shrugs his shoulders and puts the package on a nearby table, but the wide smile never leaves his face.

"Listen," I say, stepping toward the door, "I have to get back my post, but it was really good to see you, Adrian. I'll see if I can stop by again next week sometime."

"That would be *marvelous*, Mari!" He gushes, spreading his arms and spinning around.

I back out of his apartment slowly, resolving to find out all I can about these new Euphorics.

Chapter 4

"You're sure it's safe?"

"Yes, the cable will hold you," I repeat for the 10th time this morning. "Just put your feet into the loop on the bottom, hold on, and the cable will pull you up to the air barge."

The girl looks at the cable suspiciously, but finally steps into the loop.

I've been helping this year's new trainees get on to the air barge. I can't believe only two years ago it was me and my friends starting our training, excited to be getting Amplified and learning hundreds of new skills. I never could have imagined back then that I would be standing here as a Restrainer today.

"Hey, are you Mari Quillen?"

I turn around and see a young boy staring up at me.

"Yes. Can I help you?"

The boy doesn't say anything, he just continues to gaze up at me with his mouth open. This has been happening to me a lot lately. Apparently, word got out that I was the one who switched the Amplifiers back on that night of the attack. As much as the Restrainers hate me, it seems everyone else loves me. Almost every time I'm out in public, people will point at me or try to talk to me, so I do my best to stay out of sight, which isn't easy when you're wearing a metallic silver uniform.

"Okay Quillen, it's time to climb up to the barge," Clint announces as he walks by. "Say goodbye to your little admirer," he adds condescendingly. I leave the boy will his mouth still gaping and follow Clint under the aloft barge to the other side where the rest of the Restrainers are gathering. The barge is about 250 feet in the air, but the force of the turbines keeping it afloat are still strong enough to make me feel like I'm being pounded into the ground. I stumble a couple times, but manage to keep my balance so I don't fall over.

We reach the other side and each grab a cable. We have to climb them in order to get to the deck of the barge before the trainees do so we can help them over the edge. Just the thought of it makes my arms ache. I'll be climbing almost twice as high as I did when I snuck on the supply barge with Miles last year. *Good thing I'm Amplified this time*, I think bitterly.

I hear the other Restrainers giving themselves commands and I follow suit.

"Mari, climb the cable up to the air barge."

Hand over hand, I ascend the cable as quickly as I can. I glance around at the Restrainers climbing next to me. They're all climbing at the same rate, automatically, with almost bored expressions on their faces. I'm incredibly grateful when I feel the cables start ratcheting us up to the barge, but that doesn't mean I can stop. Arm strength has never been my forte, and the muscles there are already sore.

"Mari, use your legs to climb the cable," I command myself. I wrap my legs tighter around the cord and start pushing myself up with my legs, which takes some of the strain off of my arms. A Restrainer next to me gives me an odd look.

"The joints are out in my left elbow," I lie. "It hurts to use my arms."

"You can take care of that with your Amplifier," the woman responds.

"Of course! Good point," I answer, feigning relief. "I'll take care of that when we get to the barge."

The woman rolls her eyes, probably thinking about how stupid I am, but luckily she doesn't press the matter further.

I'm now moving up the cable like an inchworm. I've fallen a little behind the others, an inevitable result of my new climbing strategy. I try not to think about how much my body hurts and instead focus on how good the air feels up here. After what seems like hours I finally arrive at the deck of the barge.

We run to the other side where the trainees will be coming up, and I get slightly nostalgic as we pass the Coliseum. I intentionally take a secondary position at the edge so I'll be steadying the trainees as they come on instead of using my aching arm muscles to pull them over the side. Once the cables bring them up to the barge, it doesn't take very much time to get them all on deck and lined up alphabetically. There are a lot less trainees than I had expected.

When all the trainees are in position, a bulky man with long, stringy hair emerges from one of the nearby buildings. It's Justin, Talina's assistant trainer. Apparently, he's been promoted to head trainer. He regards everyone, making an extra effort to throw a nasty glare in my direction, and then signals that the Restrainers can leave.

I peek over the side of the barge. The landing park looks like a small, rectangular patch from up here. I strap on my goggles and smile in spite of myself.

"Mari, jump off the barge and guide your body to the landing park."

I spread my arms wide and step off the edge of the deck as calmly as I can. I hear the wind rushing through my ears as I fall through the air. It's a little unnerving to think that all I have to steer myself are the movements of my own body. I struggle to keep my eyes on the landing park below; there's so much more to look at. I see the entire Community stretching out beneath me, the eight compounds connected to the city by the Mall-cruiser tracks. Altogether, it looks like a huge spider.

I notice that I'm drifting away from my target on the landing park, so I adjust one of my hands slightly so that I float sideways. Soon I am centered again. I don't want to think about what would happen if I drifted outside of the park's boundaries. I continue to make small movements with my hands and feet, concentrating on keeping my body steady.

I'm nearing the landing park now. For a few seconds I'm afraid the air turbines aren't on, but soon I feel the resistance. It begins as a minor pressure pushing up from below and steadily increases as it slows my descent. I'm one of the last Restrainers to get to the threshold in the landing park, probably because most of the others were doing fancy acrobatics on the way down while I just kept my body outstretched. We all hover about 4 feet up until the last stage of the turbines powers down and we fall lightly onto the grated floor.

People that were watching our descent begin to disperse, and I grit my teeth and force myself to walk steadily out of the park. It's all I can do to try and keep my legs from shaking.

————-

When I finally get to my apartment building I'm startled to find that my door is slightly open. I look suspiciously down the bright hallway, but nothing seems out of place. Everything looks pristine, as usual. I had tried to avoid living in these extravagant apartments with all the other Restrainers, but it was expected. I didn't want to draw more attention to myself.

I carefully push open the door, my other hand reaching for the gun at my side. I peer into the front room. Nothing appears to be out of the ordinary, everything is where I left it. My apartment is incredibly sparse. The only things I brought here were some clothes and my ancient music device, and the apartment was supplied with only the most necessary furniture. In general, the place looks very empty.

    I creep around the corner. The door to the bedroom is cracked open and I can see that someone is sitting on my bed. My heart starts beating faster. *Who would want to break into my apartment?* I take a deep breath, then kick open the door and aim my gun at the intruder.

    He jumps off the bed and puts his hands in the air.

    "Whoa! Mari! I just need to talk to you!"

    It's Liam.

Chapter 5

I quickly put my gun down when I see who it is, but I'm still a little shaken. Apparently, so is Liam.

"What are you doing pointing a gun at my face?" He exclaims.

"What are you doing breaking into my apartment?" I fire back.

"I need to talk to you and I couldn't just stand out waiting for you in the hallway!"

"You scared me! You could have been anyone! How did you get in?"

"It was easy," he replies, a little more calm now. "I used my Amplifier. You should really think about getting more complex locks."

"Oh," I respond simply. I suddenly feel very vulnerable knowing that almost anyone could get into my apartment. "I'm sorry I almost shot you," I say, sitting down on the bed, "but you would have done the same thing in my situation."

"If I were in your situation I'd work on a better security system."

"Okay, I get it," I grumble. "Why do you need to talk to me?"

"It's Alia."

I feel an immediate heaviness in the room. I've thought countless times about how to get up to the North to find Alia, but none of my ideas seem possible. I've only been an official Restrainer for a few weeks now and I really don't have much influence with anyone. How could I expect to be approved for a costly rescue mission?

"What do you want me to do?" I ask hopelessly.

"Talk to Governor Plenaris," Liam responds.

"Look, if you think the Governor and I are on good terms just because he made me a Restrainer, you are mistaken," I argue. "He hates me just as much as he ever did, maybe even more now, and he's not going to be thrilled with me if I ask him to go find some hostages he doesn't care about."

"Maybe not the hostages," Liam counters," but I'll bet you anything he cares a lot about the technology."

I bite my lip. I had never considered that angle.

"Go on," I urge.

"If you go to the Governor and request an assignment to recover some of the North's resources, I'm sure he'd consider it."

"And I can find out what happened to Alia and the others while I'm there," I finish. "Liam, that's brilliant!"

"It's pretty standard, actually," he responds. "I'm surprised you hadn't already thought of it with all of your *enhanced abilities*," he adds jokingly.

I scowl at him, but he's right. I've been too distracted and narrow-minded lately with training and thinking about Miles. It's a sound plan. Now I just have to figure out how to get in to see Governor Plenaris.

―――-

 I take deep breaths as I climb the winding stairs to the top of the control tower. It's enough that I have to see the man I loathe during frequent Restrainer meetings, but now I have to face the Governor personally as well. I practically had to beg Clint to try to get me an appointment with him, which wasn't at all pleasant, but my reluctant handler came through. Now I'm regretting the whole situation.

 What if the Governor doesn't let me go? What if he suspects that I have ulterior motives? What if he does end up letting me go, but then requires something impossible from me? I desperately want to find Alia and bring her back - it's part of the reason I became a Restrainer - but this request could compromise everything.

 I reach the circular control room at the top of the tower which is surrounded by windows. I shudder as I recall the last time I was up here. Mostly everyone in the city was unconscious and the Governor was being held here while General Remington was attempting to kidnap the members of the Community. The two men were arguing about the West and destroying self-will. I still wonder how they knew each other.

 "Mari, it's your turn."

 I snap out of my memories and see Clint standing beside the door.

"Make it quick," he warns as I step into the room. I'm surprised when he follows me in, but I'm actually relieved that he'll be in here with me.

"You requested to see me, Miss Quillen?" The Governor remarks, turning to face me. "I hope nothing is wrong. Perhaps your duties are not exciting enough?" He suggests.

"No sir, my duties are perfectly acceptable," I respond awkwardly.

"Then what is your concern?"

"I've been considering the North-"

"The North is no longer a threat," the Governor cuts in. "After their crushing defeat several months ago, they have ceased their attacks."

"Yes, thanks to you, sir," I reply. I have to work really hard to make myself sound sincere as I complement him and not gag on the words as the come out of my mouth. "However," I continue, "I think it would be beneficial to send a constituency to the North in an effort to acquire a sample of their technology. This way, we can be better equipped to defend ourselves if they attack again." I swallow hard. I'd rehearsed what I was going to say dozens of times, but I'm not sure if I was convincing enough.

The Governor studies me and raises his eyebrows. After a few seconds, his mouth works itself into a smug smile.

"I agree," he says deliberately. "You would be willing to undertake this operation?"

"Of course."

"Good. Normally, I wouldn't give this type of assignment to someone so inexperienced, but I'm having a hard time finding anyone who wants to work with you," the Governor explains, almost gleefully. "The North's inventions could be very useful to us, and it will be good to have you out of the way for a couple weeks." He turns to Clint. "You will accompany her."

"Absolutely," Clint responds with a wide grin. I haven't seen him this excited since the time he caught a snake during training.

"A select group of soldiers will also join you," Governor Plenaris states. "Transport and provisions will be prepared. You will leave in two days." The Governor looks absently over at the screens in the front of the room. "You are dismissed."

I start to head out the door, relieved and elated that he approved my request.

"Miss Quillen?"

I turn back to the Governor, whose face is a mixture of amusement and loathing.

"Don't disappoint me."

Chapter 6

I nearly laugh out loud when Clint and I drive up to the warehouse behind the Governor's mansion and see the group assembled to go to the North. Standing in a line in their pristine soldier uniforms are Liam, Joby, Cassidy and Tristan. It will be nice to go to the North with some old friends, but something seems suspicious. I look over at Clint.

"Who was in charge of selecting these soldiers?" I ask.

"I was," Clint replies.

"How did you know?"

"I had to do a ton of research on you before I became your handler. I watched a lot of old surveillance. I know more about you than I'd like to admit. I also know you're really doing this to find your friend, but I don't really mind because it means a nice vacation for me in the North."

"I don't know that I'd call it a vacation," I say lightly. Altogether, I'm surprised by Clint's sensitivity. I'm touched that he'd choose all my friends to come with me. Well, except...

"Why Tristan?" I ask him.

He smiles slyly as he looks at the sour-faced, blonde soldier.

"I thought it'd be fun to see you get annoyed," he answers wryly. "Plus, I figured it'd be good for him to be with his sister."

I shrug. I guess Clint had to do something unpleasant to make up for being so nice. Regardless, I'm grateful for the group, even if I do have to put up with Tristan.

We walk forward to greet the soldiers. Suddenly, Cassidy rushes up to me.

"Mari! I can't believe how exciting this is!" She exclaims.

"Who gave you permission to address your superior?" Clint roars. Cassidy stops in her tracks. "Go back to your line, soldier!" He commands.

"Clint, it's okay," I mutter.

"No, it is not okay!" He yells back. "I understand that these are all your former peers, but they must respect your position!"

I watch Cassidy run back to stand with the others. Her lip is trembling.

I walk to her first and take her hand.

"Don't worry," I whisper, "He's a jerk to everyone." She nods and gives me a small grin.

I move down the line to shake everyone else's hands. Liam's eyes are shining with excitement, Joby smiles, but doesn't look me in the eye, and Tristan wrinkles his nose and pulls his hand away as quickly as possible.

"Soldiers," Clint announces, "this is a dangerous mission. We will be the first members of the Community to willingly go to the North. Therefore, it is imperative that you each accept and fulfill your duties. Follow me."

We walk around to the open side of the warehouse and my jaw drops. One of the North's oval airships is sitting in front of us, its sleek black color glistening in the sun. It's the only one of their fleet we were able to take down. I have to remind myself not to be terrified, but just the sight of it brings back awful memories.

"This ship has been reconstructed to carry passengers," Clint explains, looking pointedly at us. "Even though it nearly flies itself, we'll all need to take turns piloting because the trip will take at least 14 hours."

"You've got to be kidding me!" Tristan whines. Clint gives him a severe look that keeps him from opening his mouth again.

"Luckily," Clint continues, "the coordinates of the air ship's original location are already programmed in the console, so we won't risk getting lost."

"Wait," I say hesitantly, afraid Clint is going to blow up at me for interrupting, "if we've known the North's location all this time, why hasn't anyone gone before?"

"Because you're the only one brave enough to ask," Clint responds, snickering. "I swear Mari, if it were anyone else the Governor would have ripped their head off. I think he's got a soft spot for you. Or he wants you to die. I guess we'll find out when we get there."

———-

The inside of the ship looks like it could comfortably fit about 30 people. I remember the ships looking huge as they flew overhead, but being inside one of them makes me realize just how massive they are. There are rows of bunks along one side of the ship, with large seats and a couple small bathrooms on the other side. The control panel is simple; there are only a few buttons and switches in front of a large screen. The remotely controlled guns along the bottom of the ship were removed, and now the entire base is composed of fiberglass, allowing us to see everything as we fly over.

Suddenly we see a dense collection of buildings and houses below. They look like the ones we have in the Community, just older and empty.

"What is that?" Joby asks, looking almost frightened as he stares through the floor.

"I don't know," Tristan answers apprehensively, "there's nothing about it in my Amplifier."

I look around for Clint and see him sleeping on one of the bunks. I guess this is what he meant by vacation.

"It's probably where the North used to live," I muse aloud, remembering what I read in my ancestor's journal about how all the sectors used to be part of the Community.

"How would you know that?" Tristan remarks testily.

"She's got the enhanced Amplifier, remember?" Liam responds. "Of course she'd have access to that information." Tristan makes a face as he turns away and climbs into one of the bunks. Cassidy is piloting at the control panel, and Joby mutters something about going to check on the supplies. I walk over to the chairs and sit down next to Liam, who is looking melancholy.

"What are you thinking about?" I ask him.

He stares at the floor and waits until we've passed over the last of the mysterious buildings before he answers.

"Alia," he states, glancing up at me quickly then returning his gaze to the floor. "I can't imagine what it would have been like for her to have to fly 14 hours to the North in that cage."

I nod, recalling the brief image I saw of her and the others being carried off several months ago.

"It's all my fault, you know," Liam continues bitterly. "She wouldn't have been taken if I had stayed with her."

"What do you mean?" I ask cautiously.

"That night, when we realized our Amplifiers had been turned back on, I made Alia stay in the Mall-cruiser while I went out to see if it was safe. Turns out I left her in the worst place possible."

"Liam, if you had stayed with her, you both would have been abducted," I say, trying to encourage him, "and then who would have given me that great idea to ask the Governor about getting the North's technology?"

Liam smiles weakly, but I can tell he almost wishes he were taken with Alia.

"Hey Mari!" Cassidy calls from the front of the ship, making me jump, "It's your turn to pilot."

———-

"We'll arrive at the North's headquarters in 15 minutes," Clint shouts.

I roll out of the bunk I've been sleeping in and stare through the floor. I have to rub my eyes a couple times to make sure I'm seeing right. I must have been sleeping for a long time, because the landscape has completely changed. We're flying over jagged mountains and everywhere I look I see bright white. I assume it's snow, something I've never seen in my life except in the films we watched in school.

"We should be prepared to fight," Clint continues. "They've probably detected us already, so be ready to take action. There are plenty of weapons in the cargo hold."

I catch my breath as the North comes into view. Jutting out among the peaks are dozens of tall black buildings, probably made from the same material as this ship. They're elegant and intimidating, the black a stark contrast to the surrounding white. I finally realize how truly insane this mission is. How could I think a few of us would be able to take on a whole sector? Did I imagine we could just stroll in and take back our hostages along with a sample of their technology without suffering any losses?

The ship slowly lands in front of the largest building, which I assume is their headquarters. I grab a gun and walk cautiously out of the ship with the others. I've never felt this kind of cold before. It penetrates our thin uniforms and makes me scared to stand still, but we don't have anything else to wear. How could we have known to dress for this climate? We are the first ones to come here.

We trudge to the tall building, sometimes sinking up to our knees in the snow. Our entrance here is not graceful or stealthy. I don't want to go through the front doors, but I think at this point everyone's primary concern is just to get out of the cold. Thankfully, the doors are unlocked. We throw them open and step in, expecting the worst, but nothing could have prepared us for this.

Chapter 7

There are dead bodies everywhere. They are piled on top of each other and in varying stages of decay. The cold has kept them more intact than they otherwise would have been, but the stench is still overpowering. My skin crawls. I hear Cassidy scream behind me. Joby rushes to get away from the bodies and stumbles over one. Joby and the body slam against a wall, and the corpse makes an odd clinking sound. I force myself to look closer at the heaps of dead bodies and notice something that makes me shiver, and it's not just because of the temperature.

Under their decomposing skin I see metallic plates and hinges. Their human parts are fused with rusting robot parts. I close my eyes as I try to process this information. These people were half human, half machine.

I hear Clint access his Amplifier.

"Clint, figure out what happened to these people." He methodically scans all the bodies, then reaches down to inspect a few nearest him.

"Hm, something went very wrong here," Clint remarks.

"No kidding," Tristan says sarcastically. "You don't have to be a Restrainer to see that."

"Shut up, Prewitt!" Clint growls, making Tristan shrink back. "These people were on to something brilliant," he explains, "making themselves immortal by slowly merging technological components with their organic systems to automatically replenish the failing organs, but some event caused a malfunction that killed everybody."

"Like what?" Joby ventures, looking like he's going to vomit.

"I don't know,"Clint responds. "There's not enough information here for my Amplifier to piece that together. We'll have to explore the other buildings."

We step back outside into the freezing weather and start heading to the adjacent building. I peer up at the huge mountains surrounding us. It's beautiful here, in a desolate way. Suddenly, I run right into the back of Liam, who has stopped walking. I'm about to ask him what's wrong when I see what he's staring at. There are several sets of footprints leading to a small building about 200 feet away. Liam immediately starts running to the building.

"I know she's in there! She has to be!" He yells as he struggles through the snow.

"Wait, Liam! It could be anybody!" I shout after him, but he doesn't slow down. The rest of us hurry to follow him, readying our weapons in case we are greeted by enemies. We burst through the doors into an unassuming room with a few operating tables and dozens of blank screens. At least there aren't any dead bodies here.

We stand there in silence for a few seconds, trying to make sense of our surroundings. In the dark corners of the room, there appear to be dozens of robots similar to the ones that attacked the Community. The ceiling is covered with machinery and instruments, poised above to assist with operations on the tables below.

Suddenly, we hear a whimper come from under one of the tables. We all slowly converge on the table with our weapons ready. I crouch down and am soon staring into the wide eyes of a small boy with bright, white hair.

"Eeyah! Eeyah!" He screams.

I try to calm or hush him, but he keeps hysterically screaming that foreign word, possibly calling for help. There's a commotion as the wall behind the boy opens up to reveal a line of people covered from head to toe in long, white parkas, holding the biggest guns I have ever seen in my life.

"Eeyah!" The boy repeats, scrambling out from under the table and running up to the person in front. The figure picks the tiny boy up and throws back the hood of their parka. It's Alia.

I'm so overcome with shock and relief that I nearly drop my gun. Alia's eyes grow wider and wider as she looks at each of us, her gaze finally resting on Liam. She sets down the boy and starts toward him as he runs to her. They embrace and kiss. And kiss. And kiss.

The people that were standing by Alia remove their hoods and I recognize them as the other three soldiers that were taken. There are two boys and one girl, and one of the boys is glaring furiously at Liam and Alia who, incredibly, are still kissing. I mean, I'm glad that they've found each other again, but they're making this really uncomfortable for the rest of us.

Finally, the little boy runs over and starts pounding his fists on Liam's calves.

"My Eeyah! My Eeyah!" He shouts indignantly.

"Whoa, Liam," Joby calls out, "it looks like you've got some competition!"

They break apart and Alia again picks up the little boy, soothing him. Liam can't seem to stop smiling. Alia runs over to me and gives me a one-armed hug, squishing the little boy in between us.

"Mari," she exclaims, "I can't tell you how happy I am to see you guys!"

"I can't believe we found you!" I respond. "What happened? What have you been doing all this time?"

"Surviving, obviously," the boy with the glare interrupts, walking over to Alia.

"Oh sorry, this is Brice," Alia explains nervously. "And that's Kaylie and Trey," she adds, gesturing to the other girl and boy behind her. "These past several months have been rough, and we've all gotten pretty close."

"How close?" Liam asks, eyeing Brice suspiciously.

"Close enough," Brice responds, putting a hand on Alia's shoulder.

"Like family," Alia says quickly, tactfully shifting the little boy to her other arm so that Brice's hand falls off her shoulder. "We're so glad you all came!" She adds.

"Yeah, took you long enough," Brice remarks smugly. "We thought we were going to die here."

Alia gives Brice a nasty look, then turns back to us.

"When we were brought here, it was pretty much the same as it is now. Everyone was dead, and had been for a long time, except for Juro."

"Juro?" I ask.

"Yeah, Juro," she says, looking at the small boy in her arms who beams back at her. "He's General Remington's son."

That would explain the familiar white hair, I think.

"As far as we can tell, the General and Juro were the only ones alive out here for months, until the General went to the Community, where I assume...?"

"Yes. He's dead," I mouth to Alia. I don't know how much the little boy understands, but I don't want to risk upsetting him.

"Why didn't you guys try to get back to the Community?" Clint asks. "Surely with all of their technology here you could have come up with some mode of transportation."

"Our Amplifiers don't work here, we're outside of the boundary," Kaylie replies simply. I don't know the girl, but her response kind of makes me want to smack her in the back of her head.

Alia's mouth goes into a tight line.

"We've been busy trying to find food and warmth," she says. "Hybrids don't need either, so it's been a challenge."

"Hybrids?" Joby chokes out.

"Human robots," Alia explains nonchalantly. "Almost every building here is full of their bodies. They were trying to create the perfect combination of machine and mortal, but clearly, it didn't work out. That's why General Remington tried to kidnap all the members of the Community. He needed more test subjects."

My mouth goes dry as I think about the kind of lives we'd be living if General Remington had succeeded.

Chapter 8

"How exactly did all these people die?" Clint asks.

Alia shivers. "We found it here in General Remington's lab research," she says, turning on one of the screens in the room. The screen displays numerous diagrams and notes, with drawings of bodies and machinery parts. We all step closer to get a better look.

"Do you want to explain this, Trey?" Alia asks the soldier behind her. "It seems like you've been studying it the most."

"Uh, sure," the soldier answers quietly and shuffles over to the illuminated screen. "The citizens of the North were attempting to overcome natural death by integrating electromechanical components into the human systems. The robot parts would regenerate the body and vise versa, thus creating a self-sustaining and indestructible entity. But in order to be successful, the Hybrids had to stay under a stress threshold. If it was exceeded, the pressure of their emotions would overload the mechanical systems and destroy the entire being."

"Did they know they had to control their feelings?" Cassidy asks, looking horrified.

"Of course," Trey responds. "They went through extensive training to condition themselves to stay calm in stressful or tempting situations. But apparently, learning about it and living it were two entirely different situations."

I shake my head. I don't know if I'd want to live forever if I couldn't fully experience everything. Although, I realize that we're living it on the other side of the spectrum in the Community. We have access to the most thrilling sensations, but they're dulled by the ease of achieving them through the Amplifiers.

Even with such phenomenal resources, somehow none of us can live truly fulfilling lives.

"General Remington documented all of the Hybrid malfunctions in these videos," Trey explains, bringing up a file on the screen.

The General's face suddenly fills the screen, and Juro starts squirming in Alia's arms.

"Daddy! I want daddy!" He yells excitedly, trying to grab at the image. Alia calmly takes him around the corner where the screen is out of sight.

"Day 141 of the Hybrid Experiment," the digital General recites, looking almost bored. *"Today there was an argument between subjects 673, 29, and 307 in the dormitories of the school. The disagreement escalated and the tension overtook their mechanical functions. We are attempting to keep their deaths secret. In my estimation, they were too young. I'll propose to the council that everyone under 14 should be in isolation until they are properly conditioned."*

Trey brings up another video of the General.

"Day 179 of the Hybrid Experiment. Subjects 152 and 799 were starting to become intimate, even though it

has been made clear that reproduction is no longer necessary," he reports with a touch of annoyance in his voice. *"At least we can assume they died happily,"* he adds sarcastically. *"I'm ordering another course of sexual dilution for all the Hybrids."*

The last video that Trey opens shows General Remington looking slightly maniacal, much like the way he looked when I first saw him in our Community's control tower.

"Day 512 of the Hybrid Experiment," he says quickly. *"There was an avalanche on the East side next to the recreational area. Some were killed by the avalanche, some were killed by the exertion of running and screaming, and the rest were killed from the fear of watching the others die. I was ignorant not to account for natural disasters, but many still could have been saved had they exercised more self restraint."*

"However, this presents a great opportunity to start fresh. The citizens of the South are perfectly suited to become Hybrids. I'll weaken them by depleting their resources and then bring them here to go through the operation. Through their Amplification, they only need to command themselves to remain placid and can therefore easily stay below the stress threshold. This combination will likely allow me to finally perform the operation on myself and on my son, Juro."

The video cuts out and we all stand in silence for a few moments.

"Fascinating," Clint says finally. "Do you know where the Hybrid designs are?" He asks, inspecting the area around the screens.

"I'm pretty sure all the conceptions are in this safe," Trey replies, casually moving some robots out of the way to reveal a large black container in the corner of the room.

Clint approaches the safe and eyes it with interest.

"Clint, find out how to open the safe."

He runs his fingers along the back of the container and pulls out a transparent panel about three quarters of the way up. He etches an elaborate pattern on the panel with his fingers, and as soon as he finishes, the outer layer of the safe disintegrates to the floor, exposing a tall stand holding a tiny chip.

"This must be it," Clint announces as he plucks the chip from the stand and puts it in a small case. "The Governor will be very eager to see this."

Suddenly, Juro starts screaming. We all turn around to see what's wrong and see him clinging to Alia's leg and pointing at the ground. It takes a moment to figure out what he's pointing at, but soon it becomes clear. The particles of the disintegrated safe are crawling into the walls and into the robots in the corner. I watch in horror as the walls begin to crumble and the robots come to life.

"Everybody get out now!" Brice yells, but we've already started to flee the disappearing building. Back out in the snow, it's easy to see the path of the black flecks that used to be the lab. They're moving to the towering headquarters, and once they reach it, I can't believe what happens.

    Instead of disintegrating like the other building, the structure breaks down and reassembles into hundreds of huge, fierce-looking machines. They're about 20 feet tall with sharp claws for appendages, and they're all coming toward us, probably to recover the chip we took. In a few moments, the foreboding robots are standing between us and our only chance of escape. We'll have to go through them to get to the ship.

    There is a moment of chaos as everyone commands themselves to do something different. Liam is shielding Alia while shooting at the robots' legs, Cassidy and Tristan are running around frantically, Joby is burying himself in the snow, and Clint is climbing up one of the machines. It takes a moment for Alia, Brice, Kaylie and Trey to realize that their Amplifiers are now activated because of the far reaching signal from the transmitters me and Clint have embedded in our Amplifiers, but soon they're also in action. Everyone is doing something except for me.

    I'm standing in range of several of the dangerous robots, but none of them are attacking me. In fact, the only person they're going after is Clint, the one who has the information. I watch as all the machines converge on the one Clint has climbed on. So far, he's avoiding their blows, but with more coming, he won't last long.

"Clint!" I yell. "Throw me the chip!" He only hesitates for a moment before he digs in his pocket and tosses the case to the ground several feet in front of me. I run to grab it, and immediately the robots start moving in my direction.

"Mari," I command myself, "avoid the robots and get to the air ship."

I run past a few without getting trampled, but the closer I get to the ship, the denser the army of robots. I dart around in the snow, their clawed feet stomping all around me. Soon I'm completely surrounded. I need to get rid of the chip.

I catch a glimpse of Liam running through the ranks of robots.

"Liam, take this!" I call out as I hurl the case in his direction.

Luckily, he hears me. He doubles back and scoops up the case while the robots change direction to pursue their new target. Clint must have alerted everyone else to the plan, because soon the chip is being thrown back and forth between the nine of us. The black machines crash into and stumble over each other as they continually change course to follow the case. It would be almost comical if there weren't several of us bleeding from contact with the robots' sharp claws.

Tristan is the first to get to the ship. He steps up and struggles with the door.

"It won't open!" He cries, pulling down on the handle with the weight of his whole body. The ship must be on lock down now that it's back in its own domain and may even be in attack mode. I look around. Clint is running right beside me and several machines are behind us and gaining. And I have the chip.

"Mari," I say loudly as I slow down a little, "find out how to revert the ship to its former programming."

I lunge at the ship, but almost at the same moment the sharp claws of one of the machines dig into my leg and pull me back. I hear Clint taking over the command I just gave myself.

"Clint, figure out how to revert the ship to its former programming."

The robot that has me releases my leg to get into a better attacking position, and I take the opportunity to scramble up the side of the contraption. For now, I'm safe from its claws, but the other machines are closing in. I see that Clint has opened the ship and everyone is rushing in. I wouldn't be surprised if they left me, the situation here is far too dangerous. But they won't. I still have the chip.

Whoever is piloting the air ship flies low and plows through several of the robots that are surrounding me, knocking them over, and I'm momentarily free. I charge toward the ship. It's still so low that I don't even have to jump very high to grab on to one of the runners. The side door slides open and Brice reaches out to pull me up. But just as I'm trying to grab his hand, the ship pitches downward and I nearly lose my grip. One of the robots has attached itself to the back of the ship and is inching its way over to me.

    The ship starts to drag as more robots grab on to the sides, and I can hear screaming coming from inside. I'm wondering if I should just let myself fall to the ground when I notice that there is a massive gorge up ahead.

    "Hey! Give me a parachute!" I call up to Brice.
    "Are you crazy?" He asks, his eyes wide.
    "Just do it!" I yell.

    He disappears for a moment, then comes back and hands me a pack. I struggle to put it on with one arm, alternating my grip on the runner. After what seems like hours, we're finally flying over the gorge. I take a deep breath and let go of the ship just as one of the machines swings its claw into the place where my face used to be.

    I fall through the freezing air and attempt to twist my head around to see if the robots followed me. I can't make out much, but the black objects filling the sky above me is enough confirmation that my plan is working. *Let's just hope none of them run into me*, I think as I pull the cord to release my parachute. My body jerks as the air fills the chute, and I watch a dozen or so of the machines fly past me and crash onto the rocky floor of the gorge.

    After a few moments, I feel another tug. I look up and see that there are several hooks in my parachute, and it deflates as I'm pulled back up to the ship. I reach into my pocket to make sure I still have the chip. My fingers close around the cold case and I shudder. I'm not so sure that taking that information was a good idea.

Chapter 9

"We are certain the information on that chip is tantamount, as massive security measures had been put in place to prevent it from being stolen," Clint explains nervously with the fancy vocabulary I heard him command himself to use in the hall.

The Governor paces back and forth in front of us and eyes the chip skeptically. After we got back from the North, Governor Plenaris ordered all of us to immediately report to him. We're standing at attention in a large room of the control tower while the Governor asks us various questions. It looks like Joby, Cassidy, and Tristan might fall apart.

"Who is this?" He demands, pointing at Juro, who is hiding behind Alia's legs.

"This is General Remington's son, and to our knowledge, the only surviving member of the North," Alia responds with a slight edge in her voice.

"Interesting," the Governor says as he inspects the little boy. "We'll have to find somewhere to place him."

"That won't be necessary," Alia responds firmly. "I will take responsibility for him."

My jaw drops. I'm shocked at Alia's boldness.

"That is not your decision, young lady," the Governor spits out. "You are a soldier. Do you really imagine you'll be able to take this child with you into combat and to your other duties?" He scoffs.

"I'll find a way to work it out," Alia asserts, her eyes flashing.

They stare at each other for a few tense moments.

"You'll take him for a few weeks until we figure out what to do with him," Governor Plenaris says finally, "but don't expect to be exempt from any of your work."

"Understood," Alia concedes, but I can tell she's not satisfied.

The Governor strides over to Brice. "How did you survive up there if everyone was dead?"

"There was some food in General Remington's quarters," Brice responds. "When that ran out, we had to scavenge the other dwellings."

"Is this true?" The Governor suddenly barks at Kaylie.

"Y-yes," she stammers, looking like she might cry.

"You do realize the punishment for eating real food is loss of Amplification, don't you?" He remarks menacingly.

There are gasps from several of us. *He can't be serious. Would he really punish them for trying to stay alive?*

"Okay, fine," Brice replies, crossing his arms over his chest defiantly. Governor Plenaris hesitates. He wasn't expecting this kind of response. He was probably hoping they would all beg to keep their Amplifiers. But it's clear that Brice, who has been surviving without the use of an Amplifier for the past several months, has become more strong willed and self reliant than most members of the Community.

"Of course, since you were all instrumental in recovering the North's technology, your offenses will be overlooked," the Governor backtracks. I think this is the only time I've ever seen him look uncomfortable. Alia challenged his authority and Brice called his bluff. No wonder he seems ruffled.

"We're certainly relieved that you've all made it back from the North, we've been worrying about you for months," Governor Plenaris says flatly, making it clear that he couldn't care less that the abductees are back. "You will all be integrated back into Service over the next few days. You are dismissed."

We all start to file out of the room.

"Clint," the Governor calls out, "I'd like a word."

"Sure thing, Clarence," Clint responds. The Governor makes a sour expression at Clint's use of his first name, but doesn't correct him.

The rest of us leave the room and wait until we get to the front steps of the control tower to voice our concerns.

"He didn't seem very happy we were back," Kaylie says timidly.

"Why would he be?" Brice remarks. "There are now four of us who know more about the North than the Governor ever wanted anyone to."

"But everyone there is dead," Trey says.

"Exactly," Liam cuts in. "I'll bet he wouldn't want everyone finding out how they ended up."

"You think something like that could happen here?" Kaylie asks.

"I think there are safer places to have this conversation," Tristan states coldly, looking pointedly at me.

I should be annoyed by his suspicion, but he does have a point. As a Restrainer, my allegiance is supposed to lie with Governor Plenaris. Technically, I'm supposed to report any treasonous conversation.

Tristan stalks away and Kaylie and Trey look at me uncomfortably as they leave the group. Cassidy gives me an apologetic smile before turning around and running after her brother.

I glance over at Alia and see that Juro is asleep on her shoulder.

"What are you going to do with him?" I ask her.

"I'll leave him with my aunt when he can't be with me," she responds, stroking his bright hair.

"Alia, why are you doing this?" Liam interjects.

Alia's eyes fill with tears as she takes his hand. "I'll tell you later," she says softly. "See you guys," she calls out as they walk down the stairs together. Next to me, Brice exhales loudly.

"How long have they been together?" He asks.

"I'm not sure," I reply hesitantly, not really comfortable with talking about their relationship.

"She should be with me," he states.

"Yeah?"

"I mean, I'm glad you guys rescued us, but if you hadn't, Alia would have fallen for me eventually."

"You're probably right," I admit, "but is that how you would have wanted it? Just the four of you, alone and cut off from everything for the rest of your lives?"

"I don't know, it's kind of romantic ... " he drifts off. I raise my eyebrows at him. "All right, that would be pretty awful," he concedes, turning to face me. "How about you?" He asks abruptly. "Outside of all of your Restrainers duties do you find time to get involved with anyone?"

"Are you asking me out?"

"Yeah."

"Wow, looks like you got over Alia pretty fast."

"Not at all. When you go through a traumatic experience like that with someone, it takes a long time to forget them," Brice explains, looking wistful. "No, I just need a distraction."

I laugh in spite of myself.

"I appreciate your honesty," I reply, "but trust me, you don't want to get involved with me. I'd probably just end up trying to shoot you in the head."

"What?"

"It's a long story."

Luckily, I don't have to explain myself because Clint walks out of the tower.

"Quillen, I'm glad you're still here," he bellows, slapping me on the back. "I've got news for you."

"Okay, what is it?" I ask apprehensively. I've learned that when Clint's in a good mood, it's usually bad for me.

"You're going to prison!" He announces cheerfully.

"What?" I sputter. "But the assignment was successful and I didn't-"

"Calm down," he cuts in, "you're going there as a guard."

"Oh."

"You better get ready, the prison transport leaves in 2 hours."

"What about you?"

"I'm not your handler anymore, you're going alone."

"Ah, that's why you're so happy."

"Don't get me wrong, I loved ordering you around, but it'll be nice not having baggage with me all the time."

"Wow, thanks." I say sarcastically.

"Don't take it personally, Quillen," he responds, and I'm surprised to see a flicker of sadness in his eyes. "Now get going! You have prisoners to wrangle!"

———-

The transport driver motions for me to take the passenger seat up front. I climb up into the large van and glance back through the grate that separates me from the rest of the passengers. They're the most mild looking prisoners I could have imagined. Although, I guess you really don't have to be a ruthless criminal to be sent to prison, just act out against the Equality Movement. I remember Brexlynn telling me that all her parents did to get imprisoned was make people question the Amplifiers. They probably looked about as decent as the people behind me.

"How far is the prison from here?" I ask the driver when he gets in.

"About 45 miles," he responds. He starts the van, and we ride in silence for the first 20 minutes. We drive out past Compound A into the open desert. I take another look behind me at the prisoners sitting quietly. I suppose they're so well behaved because they are either peaceful people who made a mistake or they're Amplified people who are currently being commanded through the Override not to act out. I start to wonder how the driver knows how to get to the prison with nothing to mark the way. I guess he just uses his Amplifier.

"They used to only need two Restrainers at the prison," the driver announces, seemingly out of nowhere, "but lately they've been taking on a lot more."

"Oh really?" I respond politely, not even sure he's talking to me.

"Yeah," he confirms. "I've heard good things about you, though. I'm sure you'll be able control him."

"Control who?" I ask weakly, even though I know exactly who he's talking about.

"Prisoner 568. Miles Paxton."

Chapter 10

The most disturbing thing is that he looks completely normal. After several months of being experimented on in confinement I thought he'd look more haggard, more demoralized. But he seems almost content as I view the live surveillance coming from his small cell. His dark hair is combed, his skin is smooth, and he appears slightly more muscular than when I last saw him. It's only in his honey-brown eyes that I can see the carefully hidden rage.

The prison is basically divided into two sections: the area for prisoners who were Amplified, and the area for those who weren't. There is a severe difference between these sections. For those who were never Amplified, the cells are made of heavy steel, with numerous locks on the doors. Most of the time the prisoners are kept separate from each other, except for once a week when the guards take them all outside. They are constantly shackled and monitored, and their simple requests are rarely granted.

On the other side of the prison is the space for those who used to be Amplified. In this area, security is far more relaxed. The cells are comprised of four rooms, one prisoner in each room, with shared bathing facilities. There is one simple lock on the cell doors that could probably be opened if someone spent enough time with it. These prisoners are allowed to go outside twice a day, but no one ever goes. In fact, this part of the prison looks more like a hospital. A handful of soldiers rotate through the cells to feed the prisoners capsules and give sponge baths. The prisoners rarely leave their beds. For them, the most effective means of confinement was removing their Amplifiers.

Then there's the area where Miles is kept. A separate wing on the east side of the prison houses Miles' tiny cell. The room actually seems bigger from the outside because it's surrounded by several walls and a dozen doors, each with intricate locks and codes. Next to his cell is a large arena where the Restrainers practice using the Override on new prisoners who haven't had their Amplifiers removed yet. It's also where they've been conducting experiments on Miles.

One of the guards told me how he had fought back when they tried to sedate him in order to implant his modified Amplifier. Apparently, one of the Restrainers almost lost his leg. The special Amplifier they gave Miles is enhanced, but it only responds to the Override; he can't command himself to do anything.

In the first few trials, they tried to make him do simple things like dig holes or transport cement blocks, but he wouldn't give in to the commands. All of the Restrainers there tried, thinking he might respond differently to one of their voices, but he was too strong. He just stood there glaring at the two way mirror. So they intensified the receptors in his Amplifier. After that, he started to submit to the Override commands, but always with a degree of hesitation. Some commands he would still resist completely, like anytime they wanted him to do combat.

The guard told me they had to install holographic images to make the training more realistic, hoping it would break his concentration. It worked at first, but then he seemed to get used to it and continued to resist. I guess now they're breaking him down little by little, but not as fast as the Governor wants.

I realize I'm shaking, and I sit down on my small bed in the guard's quarters to calm myself. This is what I wanted, to get to the prison and help Miles, but I didn't realize how much it would affect me. I didn't think about how I'd have to watch them hack away at his sanity and resolve. With all of the security measures surrounding him, escape seems impossible.

I look back up at the screen showing Miles in his cell. The guard's quarters has multiple screens showing surveillance of all of the prisoners, but Miles is the most prominent. I stare intently at him for a few moments, wondering if it was really the best idea for me to become a Restrainer. Suddenly, Miles looks straight up into the camera. I scream and fall back on my bed, then shake my head at my foolish reaction. I peer into his fierce but beautiful eyes. He can't see me, he doesn't even know I'm here. Or does he?

"Marianna, you need to report to the arena for Override instruction."

I glare at the soldier standing over my bed. I hardly slept all night, and when I did, I had nightmares about Miles. It's probably unusual for this soldier to see a Restrainer sleep in, but you would too if you were up all night imagining someone you love systematically destroying themselves.

"I'll be right there," I mumble, pulling myself out of bed. The soldier smirks at me before heading out the door.

I throw on my silver Restrainer uniform and pull the unruly strands of my dark red hair back into a ponytail. The arena is not far from the guard's quarters, but I have to pass through the prisoner's area, so it makes it seem like a long walk. I hear whispers and I can feel them staring at me as I pass. I quicken my pace.

When I get to the observation room, I find a tall woman with a stern expression.

"Although you may think being a Restrainer gives you some sort of privilege, tardiness is not tolerated here," she remarks coldly.

"I understand. It won't happen again."

I turn to look through the two-way mirror and immediately feel nauseous. There are several people standing dejectedly in the arena, one is even lying on the dirt floor. I recognize a couple of them from the prison transport I came in the other day. I suppose these are the people she's going to use to teach me the Override.

"Because these prisoners are new, they have not yet had their Amplification removed," she comments, gesturing out at the subjects. "This gives us an excellent opportunity to practice using the Override, and because these prisoners are in violation of the Equality Movement, there is no need for discretion," she adds with an evil smile. She unlocks a cabinet and pulls out a silver Override machine.

"Operating the machines is fairly simple, you just have to ensure your coordinates are correct," she explains. "All of the Override machines here are already programmed to the prison's range of coordinates. In any other location, you can easily find the coordinates with your Amplifier." She runs her fingers over the buttons that cover the top of the box. "Each of these buttons represent a section within the range. If there's only one subject in the range or if you want all the subjects to perform the same commands, you can just use this large black button in the middle. Otherwise, you'll need to use the other buttons. You can also expand or decrease the size of the sections with this knob. That's all the information you need to know. From now on, it will be accessible through your Amplifier."

I swallow hard as I look back at the subjects lined up in the arena.

"Go ahead and give it a try," the woman urges, sliding the Override machine over to me. I slowly unwind the small microphone and push all the buttons that cover the area of the arena.

"Jump once."

I watch as all the people in the arena, even the one who was lying on the ground, perform a single jump together in unison. I give another command.

"Do three cartwheels."

Again, the people spring to life to complete the command.

"Try isolating the subjects," the instructor suggests.

I give a series of commands while alternating between the corresponding buttons.

"Run the length of the arena."

"Do fifty push ups."

"Spin around in circles."

"Go to sleep."

"Do a double flip twist."

"Dance."

The arena explodes into a flurry of movement as everyone carries out their forced orders. I watch the activity with interest for a few moments, but I promptly drop the microphone when I realize how much I'm enjoying this. A knot forms in my stomach, and I want to push the Override machine as far away from me as possible. My instructor gives me an odd look, but doesn't ask any questions.

"Well done," she remarks, surveying the activity through the window. "Now let's see how you do with prisoner 568."

I catch my breath as she brings up a screen displaying Miles in his cell and pushes the button for his section.

"You'll have to be forceful with your commands," she cautions. "This one is very resistant."

I try to keep my hand from shaking as I take the microphone again. This is definitely not the way I want to let Miles know that I'm here. Giving him a frivolous command through the Override is about as bad as aiming a gun at his head. I'm about to speak when the door bursts open.

"Rosheta, we need you to come handle a situation with prisoner 309," a soldier announces.

My instructor looks regretfully at Miles on the screen, then at me.

"You stay here," she directs. "Don't do anything until I get back." She follows the soldier out the door and leaves me alone in the room.

I busy myself for a while by rubbing the stub of my seared off finger, but after a few moments I can't help looking up at Miles. He's still exhibiting that careful calmness, but there's a desperation in the way he carries himself. I feel my pulse quickening as I study him. I glance over at the Override machine, the button for

Miles' cell is still illuminated. I look quickly at the door, then quietly pick up the microphone.

"Miles," I whisper hurriedly, "it's me. I'm really sorry I got you into this mess, but I swear I'll get you out of here."

I stare at the screen, afraid that Miles is going to explode in anger, but instead he does something I never would have expected. He holds his head in his hands and starts crying.

"Why can't you get her out of your head?" I hear him sob to himself through the surveillance. "She betrayed you, and yet you still think about her all the time, you still hear her voice in your mind. Why do you let her haunt you?"

I feel sick. I slowly put the microphone down and realize that the only thing that could break Miles Paxton was me.

Chapter 11

I'm startled awake by the unpleasant sound of the Governor's shrill voice in my head. At first I'm livid. He assured me that the Restrainers were exempt from the Override. But then I realize it's not a command, it's an announcement.

"Attention all Restrainer's currently posted at the prison, you are to report back to the city immediately. A transport will be there to collect you in 30 minutes."

The guard's quarters erupts into activity as all of the Restrainers get out of bed and begin packing their various belongings. I only have some clothes and my ancient music device, so I head over early to the prison entrance to wait. I have a fleeting thought about hanging back and freeing some of the prisoners, but there's no way they'd let me keep being a Restrainer after something like that and I'm not ready to give up on Miles just yet.

Fortunately, Rosheta never came back the other day to make me try and command Miles through the Override. I guess the incident she was called for was so extreme that she was excused from training me. Unfortunately, I had to watch all of the other Restrainers attempt to control Miles in the arena a few hours later.

Six Restrainers shackled him from head to foot and carried him into the arena. Then they laid him down, still bound, and ran into the observation room, remotely unlocking his shackles once they were safe behind the two way mirror. All of the precautions seemed a little extreme, especially since once his binds were opened, he just calmly got to his feet and waited. Each of the Restrainers took a turn with the Override machine. With every different command, Miles' response would be about the same. He would stand there solemnly for a few seconds and then finally give in to the order.

"Touch your hands to your feet."
"Nod your head."
"Sit down."
"Lay on your side."
"Say your name."
"Bend your knees."

All of these commands seemed like warm ups, things they'd already had him do before. This went on for a few minutes, with Miles looking like a reluctant puppet, and then the commands became more involved.

"Do a back bend."
"Crawl on your hands and knees."
"Pinch your elbows."
"Do a handstand."
"Take off your shirt."
"Sing."

It took a little bit longer for Miles to complete these commands, and each time his face would distort into a mixture of concentration and hatred. It was clear that the Restrainers were having fun with him, even though they were trying to hide their laughter. They stopped smiling when they started trying the combat commands; the commands that Governor Plenaris ordered the Restrainers to give to Miles.

"Do a roundhouse kick."

"Throw a right hook."

"Perform a spinning kick."

He didn't comply with any of them. He just stood there, his eyes intense and his body shaking from the effort of resisting. The image still haunts me.

The transport pulls up to the entrance and I climb into the very back. The other Restrainers come soon after and predictably, no one sits with me. They still don't like me. That's fine, after I saw what they were doing to Miles, I don't care much for them either.

We leave the prison and I overhear a conversation between two Restrainers in front of me.

"What do you think happened?"

"I don't know, but usually when all the Restrainers are called back into the city it's because of a Dissenter attack."

My stomach starts churning. *The Dissenters? What if my mom and Daniel are there?* I think. *What am I supposed to do? Fight them?* Hopefully they'll all be long gone by the time we get there.

My anxiety doubles when the transport pulls up to the Governor's mansion, or rather, what used to be the Governor's mansion. The massive structure is completely destroyed. All that remains are a few pillars and half of a smoking wall.

A stocky Restrainer runs up to the transport.

"They made it look like they were attacking the control tower, and most of the Restrainers in the city fell for it and are now locked up and incapacitated in there," he reports gravely. "Then they bombed the mansion and took off toward the Mall-cruiser station. A few of them were in trucks, but most of them were on foot. We're guessing they're going to try and escape on the cruisers."

We start heading in the direction of the station, and as we pull away, I see something written on the lone wall of the mansion in large, black letters.

"RELEASE MILES."

I realize this wasn't another one of the Dissenters routine missions to destroy Override machines or try to get people to renounce the Amplification system. This is a threat mission.

We get to the station just as the cruisers are departing.

"Split up and search every cruiser," an older Restrainer instructs. "I'll get the station manager to stop them from leaving."

I know the Dissenter base is closest to Compounds Q and U, so I run to the Mall-cruiser going to Compound U. Nobody follows me, which is fortunate. There are gasps and murmurs when I get on board, and I see several people pointing at me and whispering my name to their neighbor. I move through the different compartments, not sure what I'm going to do if I find any of the Dissenters. I notice most of the cameras have been disabled. Smart move, I think, smiling at the uncanny ability of the Dissenters to constantly outwit the Restrainers.

I'm nearing the back end of the cruiser when I almost trip over a loosened cover of one of the storage hatches in the floor. I carefully lift the cover and see about a dozen Dissenters wearing black helmets crouched down in the hatch. They aim their weapons at me, but suddenly one of the smaller one speaks up.

"Don't shoot! That's my sister!"

"Daniel?" I choke out, struggling to keep my voice low.

"I don't care if it's your sister, she betrayed all of us and got Miles sent to prison," a woman growls. I'm fairly certain it's Roxy. "She is the last person we need to make an exception for right now!"

But before anyone can act, I hear someone come into the storage compartment. I quickly replace the cover on the hatch and straighten up.

"What's in there?" An attractive brunette Restrainer asks.

"You don't want to know," I respond, forcing a look of disgust. "Apparently, someone is relocating some graves, and they didn't do a very good job of covering the bodies."

The Restrainer looks horrified and hurries out of the compartment. I follow her, taking one last glance at the hatch where the Dissenters are hidden before leaving.

I emerge back into the station just in time to see a bunch of Restrainers escorting a group of Dissenters out from the Mall-cruiser that was heading to Compound Q. I cringe as they start to pull off their helmets, wondering how many might be old friends or acquaintances. Sure enough, from the eight in the group, I see Blaine and Jacqueline staring angrily back at me.

"They need to be put in the holding cells in the control tower until we can take them to prison," one of the Restrainers announces.

I purposely fall behind the procession of Restrainers and arrested Dissenters heading to the control tower. I'm really not in the mood to endure more animosity from the people I used to live with. It's bad enough that Miles hates me, but I guess I didn't really think about how the decision to be a Restrainer would affect my relationships with my old friends. Hopefully this will all be over soon.

We walk through the main entrance of the control tower and step into what appears to be a party. Restrainers and soldiers are dancing around and talking loudly and happily. The whole situation seems a little bit creepy.

"What happened here?" I ask the one solemn looking Restrainer in the room. "We followed the Dissenters in here, and then they diffused some chemicals into the room that made everybody act like this," he explains. I glance around at the vacant smiles everyone has plastered on their faces. Something about it is familiar.

"Our best guess," the sober Restrainer continues, "is that the chemicals have the same composition as the new Euphorics pills."

Euphorics. I had completely forgotten about the mysterious capsules that had transformed Adrian's temperament. My distaste for the effects of the new pills grows as we make our way through the most ridiculous bunch of Restrainers I've ever seen. I'm sure they'll be embarrassed when they watch the surveillance of themselves later.

I instinctively look around at the cameras in the control tower and see that they've also been disabled. *So there will be no evidence of anything I might do in here*, I think. I'm still at the back of the group taking the Dissenters to the holding cells. I grab a soldier who's still delirious from the Euphorics chemicals.

"Where are we going?" He asks goofily.

"Just on a little stroll," I reply quietly.

"Ooh, fun!" He says, swinging my hand as we walk.

We reach the holding area and they shove all eight Restrainers into one cell. The Restrainer at the front latches the two heavy bolts on the cell door. There's a small window beyond the cells, and I lean over to the soldier I brought with me.

"Hey," I whisper, "I think I see a rainbow out that window."

"No way! I love rainbows!" He exclaims, lunging wildly through the group of Restrainers to get to the window. While everyone is focused on the chaotic soldier, I subtly undo the bolts on the cell door. I catch Jacqueline's eye. She nods her head slightly.

They finally subdue the soldier looking for the non existent rainbow and everyone walks back out to the entrance of the control tower. The Restrainers and soldiers affected by the Euphorics are sent to the hospital for detoxing.

Two hours later, when the prison transport comes for the Dissenters, they're gone.

Chapter 12

"It's just not natural! You shouldn't be taking them!"

"Something that makes me feel this good can't be that bad!"

"That's exactly why you should stay away from them! You can't rely on something else to make you happy! You are the only person who can control your feelings!"

Adrian turns his back to me and starts doing something on his Transcriber. After the Dissenter assault, I was told I had two free days before going back to the prison. I decided to visit Adrian in his office at the nutrition factory where he's doing his labor rotation this week and found a whole bag of Euphorics on his desk. After seeing how the Euphorics affected the Restrainers in the control tower, I'm even more suspicious of them.

"I guess I could try and cut back a little," Adrian admits reluctantly, still looking at his transcriber, "but it's not going to be easy. Especially since sometimes we're commanded to take them through the Override."

"What do you mean?"

"About once a week, we're instructed to take a Euphorics capsule."

"So everyone has access to them?"

"Yeah, they're pretty easy to come by these days."

"Are you sure it's from the Override and you're not just imagining it?"

"Believe me, Mari, I can distinguish from my own thoughts and someone else's words in my head," he answers testily. "And we don't complain about those commands, they're much better than some of the others we've been getting lately."

"I thought they hadn't been using the Override Program much."

"They barely used it at all after the North attacked, but now we're doing more and more every week."

"Like what?"

"We've been building up a new facility over by the hospital," he tells me. "I still don't know what it's supposed to be used for. But the worst is when we're commanded to lie still."

"What's the point of that?" I ask.

"Who knows? It started out with just a few minutes. We thought maybe it was to relax, but now it's up to 40 minutes and you can't move or even go to sleep. You just have to lie there. It's torture!"

I stare at the wall behind my brother, wondering how all these things might be connected. I'm about to ask Adrian where the Euphorics are made when another worker comes into the office.

"The machines are mixing up the Satisfy and Protein capsules again," she announces dully.

"Dang it," Adrian says, putting his Transcriber down. "I have to go check on that. Thanks for visiting me Mari, maybe you can come hang out at my apartment tomorrow night?"

"No, I'll be back at the prison," I reply, "but we'll get together soon."

I walk out of the nutrition factory and start heading toward the hospital. I want to check out this new facility that's being built thanks to the Override Program. I'm just passing the control tower when I notice something that looks slightly out of place. There are several trucks lined up along the back of the tower, but one of the trucks seems a bit different. I get closer to investigate, and see that each truck is loaded with several large bags of Euphorics capsules. The truck in question is somewhat lighter in color, and it has a few scuffs and scratches, almost like it's been used more than the others. I'd bet anything it belongs to the Dissenters.

I make a risky (and probably stupid) decision. I look behind me to see if anyone is around, and then I jump into the truck. I hurriedly cover myself with the bags of Euphorics, and I wait. It's probably only 15 minutes before someone gets into the truck and starts it up, but it feels like it's been hours.

What am I doing? I think as the vehicle starts moving over the uneven ground, *I could be going anywhere.* But I don't know when I'll have a free day again, and I can't think of anything I'd rather do than try and get into the Dissenter base. This could end in so many unfortunate ways, but it's worth it if I'm somehow able to see my mom.

It's sweltering in the back of the truck underneath all these bags with the sun beating down, but I don't dare uncover myself. Finally, we stop and I'm relieved when we start descending on what I'm pretty sure is the platform that leads to the base. I need to act quickly. For a few moments we're in total darkness, and I take advantage of the obscurity to climb out of the back of the truck and crawl beneath it. Once the platform has lowered us down to the floor of the entrance chamber I'm able to see where I can safely grab onto the undercarriage of the vehicle. I pull myself up under the truck as it drives off of the platform.

I see two pairs of heavy boots appear next to me.
"How'd it go, Jerry? Did you have any trouble?"
"Nope. I don't think anyone suspected a thing."

I hear rustling as the two Dissenters unload the bags of Euphorics and walk out of the chamber. I'm about to roll out from underneath the truck when I hear voices coming from the hallway outside the chamber. It sounds like Jacqueline and Blaine.

"I'll bet she's still loyal to the Dissenters and is planning something against the Governor," Jacqueline says. "Why else would she have unlocked our cell?"

"She probably helped us escape because she knew us and felt guilty," Blaine responds. "I'll keep my eye on her, but I don't think we should trust Mari just yet. It's because of her that Miles is in prison."

"Yeah, I don't think she did it on purpose though. She cared about him a lot."

"Not as much as he cared about her," Blaine states. "Miles spent a lot of time keeping track of her on surveillance. Whenever she was in danger, he was a wreck."

Tears are streaming down my cheeks. I do everything I can to control my breathing. It would be pretty lame if I gave myself away because I was crying.

"Well, I guess Miles has other things to worry about now," Jacqueline says soberly.

"Definitely," Blaine affirms. "I hope we can break him out, but when Felix went out to the prison, he said it was nearly impossible to get into Miles' cell."

The rest of their conversation fades as they walk away from the chamber. I'm still a little shaken from what they said about Miles, but I'm also amazed that Felix managed to get in and out of the prison unnoticed. I know he's a talented spy and stowaway, but the fact that he breached the Community's most heavily guarded structure is impressive.

I quietly emerge from underneath the truck and creep out of the entrance chamber. From the distant sounds and smells, it seems like they're having dinner. I fight the urge to sneak into the kitchen to steal some real food, something I haven't had since I left several months ago. I'm careful as I pass the surveillance room, remembering that there was always at least one person on duty. I see a man in there, but he's too focused on a screen of some people kissing to notice me walking by.

I'm just starting to go down the hallway that leads to the dwellings when I see two people coming from the other end of the hall. I casually walk into one of the dwelling rooms on my left, lucky that most people leave their doors unlocked. I'm hoping I was far enough away that the people coming didn't recognize me.

I glance around and realize I must be in Roxy's room. Her clothes are hanging in the closet and I spy some documents on the table which are addressed to her. I skim over the papers; they appear to be a report of some chemical creation. At the bottom of the page is a small, handwritten note: "dulled by Euphorics."

Suddenly, I hear someone at the door. I follow my first and only instinct and dive under the bed. Moments later, I hear Roxy mumbling to herself.

"Where did I put that message I copied from the surveillance?"

I see the lower half of her body bend down and her arms begin to reach under the bed.

"Did I put it under here?" She muses as her hands come dangerously close to brushing against my side. I close my eyes and imagine what I'm going to do when she discovers me.

"Oh that's right," she says to herself as her arms abruptly pull back, "I put it under my pillow."
I exhale in relief as silently as I can. There is some rustling of paper, and the bed springs squeak as Roxy sits to read the letter.

She murmurs it as she reads. I can only catch some of the words and phrases.

"Dear Roxanne, I was disappointed… I was hoping… but your juvenile methods… disclose the location of your base… two weeks… his surgery will be complete. Regards, Clarence Plenaris."

Roxy lets out a long sigh as she falls back on the bed. I'm trying very hard not to make a sound, but small fibers keep drifting down from the mattress and tickling my nose. Sooner or later I'm sure they'll make me sneeze. After several minutes, I hear a wheezing sound and realize Roxy is snoring. This is my chance to get out, otherwise I could spend the entire night listening to Roxy sleeping.

I slide quietly out from under the bed and get to my feet. There's still a dim light in the room, so I can easily make my way to the door. But just as I reach it, I hear Roxy calling out after me.

"You'll never get away with this, you know."

I turn around slowly, preparing to explain myself, but I see that Roxy is still relaxed on her bed, her eyes closed. She's talking in her sleep. I turn back to the door and silently slip into the hallway.

Chapter 13

It's late enough now that I think mostly everyone is asleep at the base. I move quickly down the hall until I get to my mom's dwelling. I push open the door and find my mother sitting on her bed, staring vacantly at the wall.

"Who's there?" She asks calmly, looking expectantly toward the door. "Daniel, is that you? Are you having nightmares again?"

Nightmares? I think. In another situation, I might have made fun of him for something like this, but not now. I wonder what he's dreaming about.

"Who's there?" My mother repeats, shifting slightly on the bed. I inhale sharply. I'm afraid of how she'll react when she learns it's me. Will she be angry?

Suddenly, her expression changes and she sits forward.

"Mari?" She whispers. My uncertainty fades as my mom reaches her arms out, welcoming me. I rush forward into her embrace, burying my head in her shoulder.

"Mari," she cries, "I'm so glad you're here! Are you going to join the Dissenters again?"

"I...I just wanted to see you, mom," I choke out, speaking for the first time. My mother's grip loosens a bit around me and she's silent for a few moments.

"So you're still a Restrainer?" She asks softly. I can hear the disappointment in her voice.

"Yes," I reply.

"But you haven't given away the location of our base?"

"Of course not."

"Good. The reason we haven't abandoned this place yet is because I insisted you were trustworthy, but everyone is still on edge about it."

"I promise I'll never give them that information."

"I know, but they have other ways to get it out of you."

I'm about to explain how that wouldn't be possible, but my mom changes the subject.

"Why are you doing it?" She asks earnestly.

"For Miles," I respond without hesitation. My mom sighs and takes my hand.

"Mari, I admire your bravery, but even if you save Miles, you might lose yourself."

Just then, there's a soft knock on the door.

"Felicia, are you still awake?" A woman's voice asks.

"Just a minute," my mom calls out.

She grabs my face and whispers in my ear. "Get in the closet."

I jump up and slip into the tiny enclosure on the other side of the room.

"All right Patricia," my mom says, "come on in."

"Hey," Patricia says as she enters, "we're you talking to someone?"

"Just myself," my mother answers nonchalantly, "it helps me think through things."

"Well, I just wanted to let you know that it looks like the spray we used on those Restrainers and soldiers was effective. This morning -"

"You know what Patricia?" My mom interrupts. "I've got a really bad headache. Do you mind if we discuss this tomorrow?"

"Not at all. I hope you feel better Felicia."

There's some shuffling and the door closes.

I wait a few moments before I emerge and tentatively sit down on the bed. My mom looks tense.

"You should leave," she announces abruptly. "There's a small trap door that you can climb up to next to the platform in the entrance chamber. Just make sure you cover it up with dirt after you reach the surface."

I want to stay longer and talk with my mom, but her instructions seem final. I give her one last hug and then walk out into the hallway, heading back towards the entry chamber.

I manage to make it to the chamber without being seen and find the trap door without incident. I emerge out into the cool night and start on my long run back to the city. I'm really glad I was able to see my mom, but from the way she acted when I was in the closet, it's clear that she doesn't completely trust me.

―――-

The ride back on the transport to the prison is uncomfortable, to say the least. All the other Restrainers still hate me, so I'm sitting alone in the back again, but I'm smashed up against a bunch of supplies they decided to send to the prison. I'm sore and tired from running all night, and I can't stop thinking about the things I overheard at the Dissenter base.

Most worrying is the threatening message Roxy received from Governor Plenaris. I'm afraid it was referring to Miles, that if Roxy didn't give up the location of the base in two weeks, Miles would have some type of surgery. What could that be? Aren't they doing enough to him already? Maybe they're planning to change him completely so that he doesn't resist anymore. I shudder at the thought and try to concentrate on something else. I listen to a conversation between the two Restrainers sitting in front of me.

"So they all had to have their Amplifiers replaced?"

"Yeah, whatever those Dissenters sprayed at them made their technology less effective."

"What do you mean?"

"Their Amplifiers were still working, but they didn't respond as fast or as strong as they normally did."

"Wow. I bet the Governor wasn't too happy about that."

"Not at all. Assembling those Amplifiers takes a lot of time, so now the Community's behind schedule. Some of the new trainees have to wait an extra three weeks to get Amplified."

I want to dwell on this information, which lines up with the things I saw and heard at the Dissenter base last night, but I don't have time. We've arrived at the prison and some guards are waiting for us at the entrance to give us our assignments. I'm told to go to the observation room, so I drop my stuff off in the guard's quarters and hurry over there. When I walk in, Rosheta is there to greet me.

"We need to pick up where we left off," she says casually, motioning to the arena. I look through the two-way mirror and see Miles standing alone in the massive enclosure. I expected that he'd be there, but that doesn't make the situation any less frightening. Rosheta reaches down and picks up a silver Override machine.

"It's time for you to command prisoner 568."

Restrainers 14

I reluctantly take the microphone of the Override machine, trying to find a way out of this and coming up with nothing. Even if I avoid this today, I'll have to use the Override on Miles eventually. That's part of the reason I was sent here, to try my luck on the obstinate prisoner. If Miles doesn't already know I'm here, he will now.

I stare out at Miles in the arena. If he wasn't standing I'd think he was dead. His face is slack and his arms hang limply at his sides. But there's still a fire in his eyes.

I raise the microphone to my mouth, feeling it's coldness on my lips. I can only manage to get out one word.

"Smile."

Immediately, Miles' head jerks up and he stares fiercely at the two way mirror. Before I can really process what's happening, Miles runs full speed at the mirror and slams into it. A tiny crack appears at the top. I can vaguely hear Rosheta calling for back up. He retreats several feet, then comes at the mirror again. This time, he lowers his shoulder and crashes through the glass.

In less than a second he's on top of me, pinning me to the ground. He doesn't strangle me or punch me like I imagined he would. He just glares at me. The look in his eyes hurts me more than any physical force could.

"So it *was* you I heard the other day," he whispers intensely, each word dripping with loathing. "I wasn't just imagining it?"

I can't find my voice to respond, but I give a tiny nod. Several pairs of hands appear to pull Miles off of me and out of the observation room. A few other guards have gathered to look at the damage done to the mirror and listen to Rosheta's frantic account of what happened. Luckily, no one seems to be paying attention to me. I slowly get to my feet and leave the room. I walk around the prison absently until I find an empty cell. I sit down in the farthest corner, bring my knees up to my chest, and cry.

———-

I'm not surprised when they call me to the arena again the next morning. I walk across the prison trying to suppress a feeling of dread, knowing that I'll have to see Miles again. When I walk into the observation room, Rosheta and several Restrainers are already there.

"Marianna, we need you *in* the arena," Rosheta states.

My pulse quickens as I stare through the repaired mirror. Miles is again standing dejectedly in the middle of the massive room and looks much like he did yesterday, except now he has bandages on his arms and face from where he was cut by the glass. Rosheta must see the apprehension on my face because she tries to console me.

"Don't worry, we'll have guards ready to intervene if things get too intense."

Great, I think as I step through the heavy door into the arena, *but who's going to protect me from the daggers of hatred shooting out of his eyes?*

I see Miles get tense when I walk in, but otherwise, he doesn't move. I'm instructed to stand in front of the mirror, facing him. He starts doing rudimentary movements; I can tell the Restrainers on the other side of the mirror have started giving him basic commands. He raises his arms, then touches his face, then sits on the ground, but he never takes his eyes off me.

This continues for several minutes and I'm starting to wonder what the point of me being in the arena is when Miles suddenly does something they've never gotten him to do before. He performs an intricate twisting kick followed by a punch in the air. I can't believe it. This is the first time he's done any combat maneuvers, and he keeps on doing them. I guess when he broke through the mirror yesterday to get at me they realized he *does* have an aptitude for violence, but only when I'm involved. With me present, he's not able to concentrate on holding off the Override.

Now he starts moving toward me slowly, all the while punching and kicking. I should do something, but I don't move. Maybe I'm just curious to see if he's really going to hurt me. Maybe I'm just stubborn. His fists are only inches from my face when all at once, he stops. He's trembling from the effort of resisting the commands. I allow myself a half smile, which is a mistake. In the next moment, Miles furrows his brows and lands a fierce uppercut into my ribs. Pain shoots through my body and I crumple to the floor.

A half dozen Restrainers rush in to repress Miles, but there's no need. He's distanced himself several feet away from me and is shaking with anger. I can't be sure, because the hit has made me a little dizzy, but I think I see a hint of remorse in his eyes.

———

"This time," Rosheta calls out as I'm about to enter the arena again, "feel free to fight back." There is a slight tone of mocking in her voice. I guess a lot of people were surprised that I let prisoner 568 hit me without any resistance. Some thought I was scared, others thought I was just stupid. In any case, I'm now more ostracized than I was before. Nobody really wants to get near the weird girl who has such an effect on the untouchable prisoner.

I secure the door behind me and face Miles. I've been dreading this moment ever since I was escorted out of the arena yesterday. Of course they're going to keep putting me in here with him; this is the only way they've gotten him to submit to violent commands. But I don't want to hurt Miles, and considering what he did to me yesterday, I certainly don't want him to hurt me.

I don't have time to worry about it, though. Miles has already started advancing toward me, doing some sort of martial arts combination. I take a deep breath and give myself a command.

"Mari, do a triple back handspring away from your opponent."

I flinch at the word "opponent." I never thought I'd consider Miles my enemy. I complete the back handsprings and expect to be several feet away from Miles, but instead, he's almost on top of me. I have to act fast.

"Mari, block the punch and flip him over."

I lash out and knock away Miles' fist, then grab his arm and use his forward momentum to flip him onto the ground. Immediately I feel bad, but then Miles swings his leg around and knocks me off my feet, and my regret turns into anger.

We both get quickly to our feet and face each other. Miles looks pained, and I'm pretty sure it's not from being flung to the ground just now. He aims a high kick at my head and I duck.

"Mari, knock him down."

I spring forward, wrapping my arms around his waist and throwing the weight of my whole body against him, but I might as well be trying to move a cement wall.

He reaches down and grabs my ankles, prying me off of him. Then he starts spinning me around by the feet with my face up, so I see the lights in the ceiling swirl by faster and faster as he swings me around. I think I know where this is going.

"Mari, upon release, shift your body to face downward, then tuck and roll on impact."

Miles lets go and I fly through the air, following through with the command I just gave myself. I nearly roll into the wall, but I stop myself just in time. I stand up and see that Miles is charging at me. I have to stop myself from rolling my eyes. Whoever is giving Miles these commands is an idiot. Normally, Miles wouldn't do something this stupid. Just before he gets to me I dive out of the way, causing him to smack hard into the wall and slide to the floor.

I gasp and rush over to him. It looks like he's unconscious. I bend down over him and promptly get kneed in the jaw. I stagger back, clutching my head and trying not to black out. Miles stands and looks at me apologetically before jumping up and planting both of his feet into my side. The force knocks me to the floor. The pain is so severe that I don't want to move, but I hear Miles running toward me so I manage to roll over so I can see him coming. He lunges at me, looking like he's going to flatten me with his body, so I bring my legs up and kick into his chest, sending him catapulting over me. The floor shakes a little when he hits the ground.

I crane my neck back to make sure he's okay and find him looking at me. His eyes flash. He noticed that I didn't give myself a command just now. Hopefully no one else did.

We struggle to our feet and again face each other. I'm waiting for him to act, but he doesn't move. I look over at the two way mirror. Have they decided this little session is over? I glance back at Miles. He stares at me for a few moments, then inexplicably, he smiles. It's a small smile, but it's genuine, and for the first time in months he almost looks happy. My heart soars and I smile back, but then suddenly, Miles' expression turns to fear.

His body jolts forward, but he holds himself back with immense effort. Several times his feet or arms jerk out of place, but he grunts and snaps them back to their position. His fists are clenched and his knuckles are white. He's sweating profusely and tears are streaming down his face. For whatever reason, Miles is exercising every ounce of self restraint against this particular command. Just watching him makes me feel horrible. I want to help him, but I'm afraid anything I do would break his concentration.

I'm about to run to the observation room to beg them to stop when Miles collapses to the floor. A few seconds later, the door opens and in walks the last person I want to see right now. Governor Plenaris strides across the arena, casually studying the unconscious heap of Miles on the ground.

"What was that?" I ask, nodding at Miles and trying to sound nonchalant.

"That," the Governor responds, "is something we need to work on." There is a touch of annoyance in his shrill voice. "I commanded him to kill you."

Chapter 15

"What?" I yell, my voice echoing through the arena. "Kill me?"

"Miss Quillen," Governor Plenaris answers condescendingly, "I tire of your gullibility. Obviously we would have interfered before he actually killed you. This was only an exercise to see if he would follow through with the command. Apparently, he cares more about you than I suspected."

My cheeks flush.

"Or maybe he doesn't like killing people against his will," I counter.

"Maybe," the Governor replies, but I can tell he's not convinced. "Regardless," he continues, "I need you to come with me. We have some things to discuss."

I dutifully follow the Governor out of the arena. He's fiddling with the band on his wrist which activates his personal Override system; the one he can use to control people without speaking. I feel slightly nauseous as I recall the night he used it on me, and I'm fairly certain he just used it on Miles. I hear a small sound glance back at Miles. He's rubbing his head and he looks exhausted, but otherwise I think he's all right.

The observation room is empty when we enter. I assume the Governor assigned everyone elsewhere so we could have this private meeting. I'm a little nervous that he wants to speak with me alone, but then again, I'm always on edge when I'm around Governor Plenaris.

"First, I want to commend you for your excellent work with prisoner 568," he announces, turning to face me. "He has improved more in the combative commands over the last two days than the entire seven months he's been here."

I didn't really do anything, I think. Just me standing there made Miles more susceptible to the commands. But if the Governor wants to give me credit, that's fine. I need to be on his good side for a little while longer.

"I'm interested, however, in knowing how exactly your relationship stands with our prisoner," Governor Plenaris continues. "When I received the reports of your involvement in his progress, I'll admit I was a bit surprised. I had assumed you mainly knew him as a captive knows their captor during your confinement with the Dissenters, but I took it upon myself to do a little research, and what I found was quite disturbing."

One of the screens in the observation room flickers and suddenly I'm seeing a montage of Miles and myself when we were younger. We're talking at school, playing outside, spending time with his family. I swallow hard. I knew this was going to come up sooner or later. But what throws me off is the presentation. I know the Governor likes to be dramatic, but how did he put all this together and prepare it to play on that screen? Where does he get the time to work on ridiculous projects like this?

"It seems you two were childhood friends," he sneers. "How can I be sure you aren't harboring sentiments for this boy?"

I clench my teeth. I've rehearsed this story thousands of times, and it's partly true, but I still hate having to tell it to the Governor.

"Yes, Miles and I were friends," I admit, "but then he disappeared. I was angry at first, but eventually, I just forgot about him."

"I see," the Governor replies, an odd smile tugging at the corners of his mouth. "You didn't really care that he was gone, then?"

"Not really."

"So that would explain why you were so emotional when you saw him here."

The screen changes to the surveillance of the night the Dissenters attacked the air barge. The night I saw Miles for the first time after 3 years.

My chest tightens. I'm not at all surprised that the Governor came upon this footage in his "research," but seeing it replayed like this brings back all of the sensations I felt that night.

"Why did you leave me?" I hear myself say, my younger face a mix of confusion and rage. *"You were my only friend, and you just disappeared!"*

"This is not the typical behavior of an apathetic girl," the Governor comments. "It appears you actually cared about this boy quite a lot."

"At that moment, yes," I respond evenly. "Up until that point I thought he was dead. I was surprised to see him and furious that he had become a Dissenter. Furthermore, I was exhausted that night, as well as slightly intoxicated."

"Interesting," Governor Plenaris mutters, turning to look back at the screen. "Ah, but this is my favorite part," he oozes with a cruel smile.

I force myself to watch the footage. Miles and I are conspicuously close to each other. Miles' expression is pure, sincere.

"Mari," he says, *"I had to fight. I had to leave. But you have filled my thoughts every single day since then."*

I watch him search my face and lean closer. I'm positive now that he was going to kiss me. But then I watch my body stiffen as the Override command comes into my mind. I raise my arm, aiming my gun at his head. The screen goes black, and I notice that Governor Plenaris is studying me carefully.

"It's clear that this Miles Paxton had feelings for you, and perhaps still does."

"I can assure you, the feeling is not mutual," I lie.

"And yet, you resisted the command to kill him that night."

"Yes, I did," I reply, looking the Governor in the eyes. "I also don't like killing people against my will."

"Miss Quillen," the Governor says, clasping his hands behind his back, "you have taken an oath to protect the Community and the Equality Movement. I must ask you, then, if it were necessary, would you be able to kill Miles Paxton?"

My mind races. Of course I wouldn't kill Miles, but I can't imagine that the Governor actually wants him to die - not after all the time and resources he's spent on him - that would be useless. He must just be looking for a declaration of loyalty, so I give it.

"Yes, sir," I answer, my mouth going dry as the words come out.

"Excellent," he says, smiling and relaxing a little. "Now, I need you to gather your things and report to the entrance in 10 minutes. You will resume your work with the prisoner next week when you return."

"Return from where?"

"Your team did such an excellent job gathering information from the North, I'm sending you all to investigate the East."

"What's in the East?" I ask, a little bewildered that he would suddenly take an interest in the withdrawn sector.

"That's what I'm sending you to find out," he replies, almost cheerfully. "We didn't take action against the North soon enough and they almost destroyed us. I would like to be forewarned if the East is conspiring against us."

I'm speechless. Sending us to the East seems like a rash and haphazard decision, especially since most of the Community doesn't even know that the East exists.

"Hurry up," the Governor urges, turning to leave. "Your transport will be leaving soon."

The Governor walks out of the observation room, and I look back out at the arena. I almost scream as I see Miles standing just a few feet away, staring at the mirror, his face ashen. I glance down at the Override machine on the counter and see that it's still on, the microphone unraveled and activated. Miles heard our entire conversation.

Chapter 16

"Do we even know where we're going?"

"Nope, that's the fun part."

Tristan stomps away in frustration as Clint enthusiastically studies a map on his Transcriber. We're all loading up the air ship, the one we acquired from the North. We're taking a lot of supplies because we don't know how long it'll take to find the East.

Mostly everyone is excited to be going on this assignment, except for Tristan, of course, and Alia is a little worried about being away from Juro for so long. Otherwise, there's a general feeling of cheerful anticipation, even though it's likely that this mission will turn out to be incredibly dangerous.

We had to have a quick briefing on the East yesterday, most of us only had a faint idea that the sector even existed. There wasn't much to learn, just that they separated from the Community during the Equality Movement because they chose equality through physicality over equality through ability. It was pretty much what I already knew from reading my ancestor's journal. Still, Cassidy was so overwhelmed when they gave us the details that she almost cried.

I glance around as we make our final preparations to leave. Alia and Liam are talking quietly next to the entrance of the ship, Joby is trying to stop Cassidy and Tristan from arguing over a box of extra clothing, and

Brice is pointing something out to Clint on the Transcriber. Brice and Alia were added to the expedition because of all the survival experience they gained while they were in the North. And because Brice persuaded Clint to let them come. I'm hoping Brice doesn't try anything with Alia. The last thing we need on this trip is added drama.

"It seems like the smartest thing to do would be to visit the area where the East used to be before they split," Brice tells Clint. "That way, we might find some evidence as to where the new settlement could be."

"That's a solid idea," Clint replies.

I agree. Having a set destination is far more reassuring than just launching off and wandering in a vaguely Eastern direction. Cassidy sets down a crate of capsules and walks over to me.

"Remind me why we're trying to find the East again?" She asks.

"The Governor wants to make sure they're not planning to attack us," I respond automatically, but I can't help but feel that maybe the Governor has ulterior motives.

"Weird," she comments. "Seems like he should have tried to figure that out a long time ago."

"Yeah, maybe he's been busy with stuff," I say. *Like attempting to turn Miles into a killing machine,* I think darkly.

"Come on guys, let's get going!" Clint yells, motioning for everybody to board the air ship. "I could go by myself, but your inferiority might actually be useful," he adds.

"Do I really have to go?" Tristan whines.

"Yes," Clint responds, but I can tell he's considering leaving him behind.

We carry in the last of the supplies, set the auto pilot coordinates and take off. I peer through the transparent floor as we fly over the city and notice the new structure Adrian mentioned they were being forced to build with the Override. I'll have to check it out when we get back. I'm watching the rest of the Community pass below us when I feel a hand on my shoulder.

"How have you been?" Brice says, smiling down at me. "Is prison life as exciting as they all say?"

"Who says that?" I ask, turning slightly so that his hand falls off my shoulder.

"I do," he responds easily, not at all deterred.

"It's pretty draining, actually," I concede. "How about you? Was the Community as wonderful as you remembered it?"

"No," he responds. "I never realized how lame people are. They never take responsibility for themselves."

"What do you mean?"

"Whenever somebody makes a mistake or can't do something right, they always blame their Amplifier. It's never their fault."

"This happens a lot?"

"All the time," Brice asserts. "But anyway," he says, lowering his voice, "I have a question about Alia."

"No," I answer quickly.

"You don't even know what the question is!"

"Look Brice," I say, "I don't know what happened between you two in the North, but she's clearly chosen Liam. You seem like a great guy, but I don't think you have a chance with her."

Brice takes a deep breath. "Wow. You are very blunt."

"It must be my Amplifier," I joke. Brice smiles a little.

"But what if ?—"

"Hey Brice!" Clint calls from the front of the ship. "I need your sharp eyes to take a look at this!"

Brice shakes his head as he goes over to help Clint. Maybe I was a little too direct with him. Although, some harsh words might just do him some good.

I look around the ship. Cassidy is absorbed in counting out Nutrition capsules. Tristan is sitting next to her, absently unraveling thread from a shirt. Liam and Joby are asleep, and Alia is staring at the floor. I walk over and sit down next to her.

"How is everything with Juro?" I ask gently.

Alia's face lights up. "Mari, it's wonderful," she exclaims. "I was so empty before, but now I feel like my life has purpose, you know?"

I don't know, but I nod my head anyway.

"I'm just worried the Governor's going to take him away," she continues. "It's been a few weeks, but I doubt he's forgotten about him."

"Maybe I can help keep the Governor distracted," I remark, figuring that if I actually succeed in my plans, Governor Plenaris will have much bigger things on his plate than relocating General Remington's son.

"How are you doing?" Alia asks.

"I'm okay, I guess," I respond. "Although the prison can be really depressing sometimes."

"You've been at the prison?" Alia says intensely, suddenly very interested. "Have you seen Prisoner 568?" She whispers.

"You mean Miles Paxton?"

"So it *is* Miles," she remarks, nodding to herself. "I had heard rumors that he was captured. Is he as terrible as everyone says?"

"No, it's just Miles," I reply, wondering why Alia is talking about him like this. "You remember him, right? He was in school with us before he disappeared."

"Yeah," Alia responds, "but he always seemed really weird to me. I'm not surprised he turned out to be a maniac."

"He's not a maniac!" I protest.

"Mari, why are you defending him? He's trying to bring down the entire Community."

"Well, maybe he's not the bad guy."

"That's a pretty bold thing to say, especially coming from a Restrainer."

She's right. Even though Alia is my friend, I can't talk openly about Miles with her.

"We're told to look at every side of a situation," I explain weakly.

Alia looks like she might say something, but suddenly the air ship's navigation system starts beeping. We're just minutes away from the East's former settlement.

We land next to a slender building that may have been red at one time, but now it's a pale, sickly pink. The area looks about like our city, except instead of cement everything is made of metal, and there's more foliage. It seems like there are roots and vines growing over every structure. We all walk off the air ship tentatively, uncertain of what we're looking for or where we should go. We move slowly in between a row of squat buildings.

"That looks official, let's try in there," Joby says, pointing to a large stone building off to the left. Inside the building we find several rooms full of chairs and desks. This must have been a school. We wander into an auditorium that has a large screen at the front. Clint investigates a podium at the back and manages to turn on the projector.

Suddenly we're accosted with bright, colorful images in what appears to be an old propaganda film. Men and women wearing tight, shiny outfits and inordinate amounts of loud makeup dance around and all recite the same, insipid line.

"Who needs ability when you can have beauty?"

I don't want to jump to conclusions, but I'm fairly certain these people, if we ever find them, would not be interested in attacking us.

"What's that noise?" Cassidy yells above the sound of the propaganda film. Clint switches off the projector, and at first, I hear nothing, but after a few seconds I notice a faint rumble. We rush outside of the school to try and see where the noise is coming from. We can't see anything, but the rumbling is getting louder. I run up the front steps of an adjacent building to see if I can get a better view. What I see off in the distance almost makes me fall over.

"Get in the ship!" I scream as I stumble down the steps. The others don't question me. They take off running. The ground begins to shake and I glance behind me. The first wave of the stampeding beasts appears at the far end of the street. I will my feet to run faster. I'm about 20 feet away from the ship when out of the corner of my eye I see horns. I recognize these creatures from when we tagged animals in the Preserve during Training. Buffaloes.

    Clint is already getting us off the ground when I dive through the doors of the air ship. The buffaloes run all around us and occasionally run into the side of the ship, but they don't do much damage. Once we're in the air we can see thousands of them trampling through what used to be the East, smashing through the old structures and tearing up the landscape. If there was any evidence down there that could lead us to the new sector, it's probably destroyed now.

Chapter 17

"Where did those animals come from?" Tristan exclaims, inspecting a scrape on his elbow.

"They must have escaped from the Preserve, it's about 10 miles north of here," Clint answers. "The real question is how? That place has more security than our prison."

"Do you think we should go over and check it out?" Joby asks.

"That's not our assignment," Clint responds. "We'll just have to report it to the Governor when we get back from the East."

We all look at each other uncomfortably. We're aimlessly drifting eastward, and we're essentially back where we started with no clues as to where we'll find the East. I gaze through the ship's floor at the landscape below, remembering that there used to be guns on the bottom of the ship before we removed them. Suddenly, I have an idea.

"Hey, does this ship still have its weapons communication system?"

"Yeah," Tristan replies, "It's in the ceiling of the secondary cargo area."

Everyone stares as him.

"What?" He says defensively. "I explored the whole ship. It's something any *normal* person would do when stepping onto an air craft that was previously owned by our enemy."

"Fair enough," Clint responds. "But how is this supposed to help us?"

"Every time we were attacked by these air ships, the weapons would target crops and buildings, but never people," I explain. "We know now that the ships were probably controlled by just one person, General Remington, and there's no way he could have manipulated all the ships individually. So there must have been a feature that allowed the weapons to pinpoint specific elements or materials."

Clint starts to catch on. "If we could activate that system and program it to locate a specific material…"

"Like metal," Cassidy pipes up, "most of their old buildings were made out of metal."

"Then the ship would take us toward that substance!" Clint finishes excitedly. "Tristan, show me where that system is."

Clint and Tristan disappear into the storage area. A few moments later, they come back up. Clint's eyes are shining.

"We've found the East."

———-

Five hours later, we pass over a mountain range and are nearly blinded from the reflection of the afternoon sun off of hundreds of buildings below us. At first I think it's glass, but as we get closer I squint and see that all the buildings are completely covered in mirrors. We might have been able to find this place if we had known the general vicinity, you can probably see the glare from 50 miles away.

We prepare our weapons and cautiously walk off the ship, but I still don't expect these people to be very violent. Walking out into the East is like entering a complex maze. With all the mirrors, it's hard to tell which ones are the real buildings and which ones are the reflections. Everywhere I look I see myself from every different angle. It's a little unnerving.

All the streets seem to be leading to a tall, circular building. We approach the massive double doors and stand there for a few moments, staring back at our reflections.

"I'll go in first to make sure it's safe," Clint volunteers. He slips slowly through the doors while we wait outside. I take a look around. The streets and sidewalks are all clean, and every structure is immaculate. Altogether, the place is pristine. And empty.

There's something about all this that feels eerily familiar. Joby must notice it too. He looks sick.

Suddenly, Clint pops his head out of the door.

"Guys, you've got to come see this," he says.

"Don't tell me they're all dead and decomposing," Joby moans.

"Well, they're not decomposing," Clint replies.

We walk through the doors and down a dark corridor that opens up into an immense, circular chamber, lined from top to bottom with thousands of the most beautiful dead people I've ever seen. They're all on display in glass cases, standing upright and dressed in various bright fabrics. Their faces are mesmerizing and their bodies are very impressive.

I walk around and examine the corpses. Whatever technology the East had allowed them to achieve physical perfection. They all have perfect skin, prominent cheek bones and jaw lines, large, bright eyes, thick hair, and amazing proportions. Every once in a while I'll catch a glimpse of my own reflection in the glass and I'll be startled by my lanky frame and unkempt red hair.

On the bottom of every case is a plaque with the person's name on it. Underneath the name, where you might expect some of their achievements or a message about their loved ones to be written, there is a list of their measurements and features. Height, weight, eye color, waist size, and so on. It all seems a bit hollow.

Alia comes up next to me as I'm studying a very attractive man with broad shoulders.

"I almost wish I could have lived in the East," she whispers, staring into the man's huge green eyes.

"So you could end up like this?" I respond.

"Yeah, I guess that wouldn't be ideal," Alia concedes, taking in all of the lifeless figures in front of her. "I wonder what made them do this?"

"They wanted to be preserved at their peak," Clint says suddenly. I jump. I hadn't noticed that he was behind us.

"Was that information in your Amplifier?" I ask.

"No, it's in this pamphlet," he responds, holding up a booklet with a woman's face on it. "There were a bunch of these at the entrance."

"What else does it say?" Liam asks as he walks over.

"Basically that they would rather die beautiful than have to watch their bodies break down as they aged. So they all killed themselves by ingesting an incredibly powerful preservative, and now we have this museum of gorgeous cadavers."

"So they all just died out?" Brice exclaims. "They didn't reproduce?"

"Of course not. Who would want to ruin those figures?" Cassidy remarks, gesturing to a row of women with tiny waists.

I blow my hair out of my face in bewilderment. The North didn't want to lose their resources and the East didn't want to lose their beauty, and they both ended up wiping themselves out. How much longer do we have before our thirst for ability destroys us?

"Well," Clint announces, "let's get out of here. This place is giving me the creeps." We start to walk out of the chamber, and I see Clint slip something into his pocket.

"What was that?" I ask him.

"A souvenir," he responds, winking at me. I don't press him further. It was probably just the pamphlet.

I turn around and take one last look at the stunning mausoleum. I'm pretty sure I'm going to have nightmares for weeks.

Chapter 18

Governor Plenaris didn't have much to say to us, probably because we didn't have much to report. The briefing lasted about 10 minutes, and while he was surprised that everyone in the East is dead, he really didn't seem to care much. I guess to him it's just another few thousand potential enemies crossed off of his list.

Now I have three hours before my transport back to the prison leaves. I stop by my apartment and find I have an Adhesive waiting for me from Adrian. I lay down on my bed and apply the small strip to my temple.

The video message takes effect and I'm immediately surrounded by one of the recording rooms in his apartment complex. Adrian appears in front of me. He looks tense.

"Hey Mari," he begins, trying to force his mouth into a smile but failing, *"I hope everything is good at the prison or wherever you are. They told me you're unreachable right now. When you get back, could you come see me? I need to talk to you. I'm doing my labor rotations in the research facility this week."*

Adrian and the room fade as the Adhesive dissolves into my skin. I wonder what has him so worried and why he was so cryptic. Maybe what he wants to talk about is contrary to the Community or the Equality Movement. In any case, if it's bothering Adrian, it must be really bad.

I make my way over to the research facility, a small, angular building next to the control tower. It's easy to spot Adrian when I walk in, his massive frame is filling up one of the examination booths that line the back wall. I step past two people throwing a magnetic disk back and forth and approach my brother, who is hunched over a microscope and several trays of Euphorics capsules.

I watch him for a few minutes. He's completely absorbed in studying the pills. He'll take a capsule from one of the trays, then give himself a command.

"Adrian, determine the composition of this capsule."

Then he'll take the capsule and put it in one of two boxes on the floor next to him. I let him get through about 10 capsules before I finally walk up behind him.

"This looks really exciting," I say right into his ear. He whips around, nearly knocking over the microscope.

"Mari!" He exclaims. "Don't do that! You scared me!"

"Sorry," I respond lightly, not bothering to hide my amused expression. "How's it going?"

"Not good," he admits, glancing around to see if anyone is close enough to hear. "Some of the Euphorics capsules were modified," he whispers. "Everyone who took the modified capsules are having trouble with their Amplifiers."

"What do you mean?" I ask, but I think I already know the answer.

"They're still working, but they're not as strong. The Amplifiers will only pick up half of the commands given to them, and sometimes they'll just stop working in the middle of a command."

I press my lips together as everything falls into place. The load of Euphorics stolen by the Dissenters, the "dulled by Euphorics" note scribbled in Roxy's dwelling... this is the Dissenters strategy for weaning the Community off of the Amplifiers, and quite frankly, I think it's genius. It was a shock to everyone to suddenly have their Amplifiers shut off when the North's robots attacked several months ago, so the Dissenters are breaking them down gradually. It's still going to be unpleasant, but it's a much more effective system than just destroying everything all at once.

"So you weren't affected then?" I ask Adrian.

"No," he replies, "You actually convinced me not to voluntarily take Euphorics anymore. That's why they've assigned me here, to find and dispose of all of the modified capsules. Everyone who's Amplifier is defected has been assigned to the more menial labor positions. They'll probably have their Amplifiers replaced eventually, but that could take up to a year. In the meantime, things are starting to fall apart. With all the people affected, there just aren't enough qualified workers to fill the more complicated labor positions."

"I can imagine," I remark.

"Did you know something about this?"

"No," I reply carefully. Technically, I didn't figure it all out until just now.

"It's just that you were so insistent about staying away from the Euphorics, I thought that maybe ... " he trails off.

"Adrian, I was against them because they altered your mind in a really unsettling way." I state.

"I guess that makes sense," Adrian concedes. "But what I really want to know is why they aren't getting rid of the Euphorics altogether? Why are we still getting commands through the Override to take them?"

It's a good question, but I don't get to discuss it with him because suddenly he drops his equipment and lies down on the floor. His eyes are still open and looking at me, but otherwise, he doesn't move. I'm about to try to get him back up until I notice that almost every other person in the research facility has done the same thing. The one guy who's not lying on the floor shrugs his shoulders at me and then returns to work. It must be the Override commanding them to lie still like Adrian was telling me about before. I don't know how long this is going to last, so I awkwardly wave goodbye to Adrian and walk out of the facility, stepping over a few people on the floor in the process.

From the outside of the research facility I can just see the corner of the new building they've been constructing behind the hospital. I still have a little time before the transport leaves so I decide to go check it out. On the way over I see dozens of people who have stopped whatever they were doing and are lying still in the streets and on the steps of buildings. I notice a few of them looking at me and feel very conspicuous to be the only person moving around in the area.

    I get to the building and am surprised to see that it's almost finished. They must have been using the Override Program for it even more than Adrian had mentioned. It's large and rectangular, and it looks like it's two stories tall. The front door is propped open so I walk in. The inside is nothing more than one massive, empty room. It looks like there might be something on the ceiling, but it's so dark that I really can't tell.

    I can't imagine what the Governor is planning to use this for, but the blatant nothingness of it makes me shiver. It doesn't seem like anything special, but that's what frightens me the most.

Chapter 19

When I walk into the prison, I don't see a single guard. There are no guards in either of the prisoner sections and the guard's quarters is completely empty. I finally see a guard lounging in a chair in the hallway smiling stupidly.

"Hey, where is everyone?"

The guard jumps up. "What?" he exclaims, then calms down a little and says, "Sorry, I didn't see you coming and you scared me. I'm watching a movie." He adds as he touches the Adhesive applied to his temple. "We got a bunch of new prisoners in today, so, you know…" he says slyly and winks at me. I have no idea what he's talking about, but I don't think he's going to be very helpful with his optical and auditory systems occupied by the Adhesive movie, so I keep walking down the hall. As I near the arena, I start to hear animated shouting. I break into a run, afraid that Miles is in trouble. I throw open the door to the observation room. Miles is nowhere in sight, but the scene in front of me makes me just as nauseous.

A dozen guards are crowded near the two way mirror, each clutching an Override machine. In the arena are the new prisoners that haven't had their Amplifiers removed yet, and they're all viciously fighting each other according to the guards' commands through the Override machines. It's hard to make out all of the commands, they're giving them so fast.

"Kick three people in the head."

"Knock the woman closest to you off her feet."

"Elbow the man to your right in the jaw."

"Run to the other side of the arena."

"Headbutt your neighbor."

"Roundhouse kick the tall one."

"Punch everybody else in the face."

It's a violent mess of arms and legs as each prisoner tries to complete their commands while getting pummeled on every side. A few other guards are watching the spectacle and taking bets on the winner. It's a disgusting display of misusing the Override, but I realize this is a perfect distraction. No one is paying attention to Prisoner 568 safe and alone in his cell.

I slowly make my way over to the control panel on the back wall and shut off the screen that shows Miles. I slip out of the observation room and walk down the narrow hallway that leads to the isolated cell. The keys and codes to all of the secured doors are locked in a case next to the first gate. The case can only be opened with a classified badge. Luckily, as a Restrainer, I have one of those badges.

It takes a while to get though all of the doors, mainly because I have to keep guessing which key or code goes to which door. When I get to the last door, there's no lock or keypad, just a screen flashing the word: "IDENTIFY."

I tap the screen to see if it will show me any other instructions, but nothing happens. I place my hand on it, wondering if it wants to scan my fingerprints, but it just keeps flashing its cryptic message.

"Mari, figure out what this thing wants," I mumble. It comes to me as I notice a small microphone attached to the side of the screen.

"Marianna Quillen, Restrainer," I announce. The screen starts shifting through thousands of pictures and I feel an electrical current sting me behind my ear where my Amplifier is embedded. Finally, I hear the door unlock and slide to the side, revealing Miles sitting on his small cot and staring at the floor.

My heart aches a little to see him so vulnerable. His dark hair is a little unkempt and his broad shoulders are sagging with fatigue. When he finally glances up at me, his honey eyes burn brightly for a moment, but then go dim.

"What do you want?" He says flatly, straightening up a little.

"I'm breaking you out," I respond, trying not to show how much his tone hurts.

"Is that right?" He asks doubtfully. "How do I know this isn't part of your plan to kill me?"

"Miles, I would never kill you," I say softly.

"That's not what you told your friend Governor Plenaris," Miles retorts. "I guess you'll do anything for a little extra ability and position in the Community."

I exhale. I can understand why he's upset with me, but I think he's being a little childish.

"It's not what you think, Miles. I can explain once I get you out of here."

Suddenly, Miles leaps up from his bed and faces me.

"Why do you even care?" He shouts, his voice trembling slightly. "You've clearly never had feelings for me. Why does it matter to you if I'm free or not?"

I stare at him as I realize that of everything he overheard from my conversation with the Governor, my agreeing to kill him wasn't what hurt him the most. I step closer to him and look straight into his eyes. A lump forms in my throat.

"Don't you know me at all?" I ask, reaching out to take his hand. He tries to pull it away, but I hold on to it until he relaxes. "I need you to trust me." I whisper.

"It's hard to trust someone who keeps switching sides," Miles responds harshly, but I can tell he wants to believe me.

"We can talk later, but right now, we need to go," I affirm, trying to lead Miles out the door. To my surprise, he steps back and again sits on his cot.

"I can't," he admits, looking defeated. "If I set foot outside the prison, my Amplifier will explode and I'll die."

"What?" I exclaim. How did I not know about this feature of his modified Amplifier? I look down at the bundle of keys in my hand. *I guess we'll have to do this the hard way.*

"Okay, hold still," I instruct Miles as I approach him from behind. I begin to jab one of the keys into the skin below his ear, but in the next moment, Miles whips around and smacks my face with the back of his hand, sending me toppling to the floor. I groan as I get to my feet.

"My Amplifier is also programmed to make me attack whenever someone tries to remove it," Miles explains, wincing as he inspects my face. "You should have seen what happened to me when I tried to take it out myself," he adds, smiling weakly.

"Why didn't you tell me that before?"

"I figured that information would have been in your enhanced Amplifier," he answers bitterly.

Suddenly, an alarm starts blaring. They must have noticed the keys to Miles' cell are missing. I groan and take one last look at Miles, then bolt out the door. I rip off and smash the screen just outside of the cell, hoping they won't be able to recover the evidence of my voice from it for a while. I race through the rest of the doors, but when I get back out into the hallway I can hear someone coming. I have the keys in my hand and nowhere to go. I can only think of one way to get out of this.

I collapse to the floor just as two guards come around the corner. I clutch my head in the place Miles just hit me as they run up to me.

"What happened?" One of them asks.

"I ran over here when I heard the alarms, and some guy blasted out of the door and attacked me," I tell them shakily. "I was able to get the keys from him, but he hit me pretty hard in the head."

"Who? What guy?" The guard asks.

"The Dissenter," I lie. "He went that way," I add, pointing down the hallway. The two guards take off in that direction. I exhale. It looks like I've gotten away with it this time, but sooner or later they'll find out it was me who unsuccessfully tried to release prisoner 568.

Chapter 20

The next few days are agonizing. Everyone is baffled by the mysterious Dissenter who managed to sneak in and out of the prison's most secure cell and only be seen by one person. I've been interrogated several times, but the bruise on my face is enough to make people believe my story. In the meantime they've doubled the security on Miles' cell. So that, along with the fact that his Amplifier will kill him the minute he leaves the prison, makes rescuing Miles pretty much impossible.

On top of all this, Miles is becoming more susceptible to the Override. I no longer need to be in the arena with him for him to succumb to the violent commands. He'll only hesitate for a moment before he starts to fight someone. He's breaking down quickly and I'm afraid that soon he'll be ready for whatever the Governor has planned for him.

I'm sitting on my bed in the guard's quarters, racking my brain for some way to safely remove Miles' Amplifier. A bulky guard walks in.

"Hey Quillen, we need your help with a prisoner on the west side," he states.
"I'll be right there," I reply.

I walk through the prison, glancing occasionally into the cells of those who were never Amplified. They look restless, pacing back and forth in their cells or doing various exercises, perhaps to pass the time more quickly.

It's a stark difference when I enter the area of the prisoners who used to be Amplified. They're all laying on their beds, staring blankly at the ceiling. The only prisoner who isn't catatonic is surrounded by guards. I'm assuming this is the prisoner I was called here to help with. As I get closer I see that he's thrashing around and wailing about something.

"Please don't take them away! They make me feel so good!" He howls.

I rush forward to help restrain the anguished prisoner and see that one of the guards is holding up a large bag of Euphorics.

"Where did you get these?" The guard demands, shaking the bag in front of the prisoner.

"I can't tell you! She'll kill me!" The prisoner responds in agony.

One of the guards next to me twists the prisoner's leg.

"Ah! Okay, okay I'll tell you!" The prisoner yelps. "It's Lucy Jilkson! She brought them in for me! But please don't punish her! She's so nice!"

The guard with the Euphorics sighs. "We'll have to confiscate these," he states.

"I'll take care of them," I volunteer quickly. All of the other guards glare at me. They were probably hoping to keep them for themselves, but nobody dares to say anything. The guard holding the bag reluctantly hands them over to me, and I start heading in the direction of the trash receptacles. I hear the prisoner voicing his pathetic protests as I leave the area.

    My mind is racing. I glance behind me to make sure no one is watching, then I change my course and head toward the Nutrition dispensers. It's 5:30 right now, and 6:00 is usually when everyone breaks for evening Nutrition. The Euphorics look pretty much like the regular Nutrition capsules, except that they're a bit larger. You really can't tell the difference unless you see them next to each other. If I can switch them in the dispensers, I could create another opportunity to get Miles out. I'm still not sure what to do about his Amplifier, but I've got to take this chance.

    I reach the dispensers and luckily, there's only one other guard in the vicinity. I pretend I'm getting a capsule from the Nutrition dispenser, but instead, I reach in the bag and grab out a Euphorics pill. I turn to the guard in the room.

    "Hey, do these Nutrition capsules taste weird to you?" I ask her, holding out the Euphorics pill.

    "They seem fine to me, but let me see," she says, taking the capsule from my hand. A moment later, she's smiling idiotically and singing to herself. I quickly empty out the Nutrition dispenser and fill it with the Euphorics. Now I just have to wait and see if it works.

    I go back to the guard's quarters, too nervous to watch things play out by the dispensers. About 40 minutes later guards start wandering in, happily flinging pillows around and jumping on the beds. I run over to the arena, trying to contain my excitement. When I get to the huge enclosure, I can hardly believe what I see.

The arena is full of guards running around, doing cartwheels, rolling on the floor, hugging each other, and just generally acting absurd. I step into the observation room and find Rosheta there, gleefully pushing every button she can find.

"Mari!" She calls out, grinning goofily, "Your hair looks amazing today!"

"Wow, thanks!" I respond, trying to match her level of silliness. "Your hair looks great too!"

"It does, it does," she replies with a giggle.

"Do you know what would be so much fun?" I ask her.

"No. What?"

"Let's bring Prisoner 568 into the arena!" I announce, clapping my hands stupidly.

Rosheta's face becomes grave and I'm worried that I said the wrong thing.   But then her eyes grow wide and she smiles.

"That would be... amazing!" She yells and promptly runs out of the room. I watch her get through all of the added security measures to Miles' cell on the surveillance. Miles looks confused when she blissfully pulls him out of his cell, and even more bewildered when she brings him into the arena. She runs off to join some people holding hands and spinning around in a circle, leaving Miles alone to try to make sense of the circus happening around him.

I'm thinking the best course of action now might be to turn off all the power when I notice the Override machines on the floor. *Of course! How did I not think of this before?*

I place one of the machines in front of me and turn the knobs until I've isolated Miles. I unwind the microphone and bring it to my mouth.

"Come to the observation room."

Miles snaps his head up to look at the two way mirror. Despite his stubborn expression, he walks out of the arena and seconds later comes through the door.

"Mari, what's going on?"

"It's Euphorics."

"What are Euphorics?"

I'd forgotten Miles has been cut off from the Community for the past several months.

"It's a long story," I reply. "Basically, all the guards are useless right now." I grab a pen from the desk, hoping it's clean. "Here," I say, handing Miles the pen, "sorry there's nothing more sophisticated to use."

"What are you talking about?"

I don't explain. We don't have time. I raise the microphone of the Override Machine to my mouth again.

"Remove your Amplifier," I command.

Miles' eyes light up as his hand automatically reaches up and stabs behind his ear with the pen. He looks relieved even though I know it's really painful to be digging into his own skin. When he's completely opened up the site, I give another command through the Override.

"Break the chip before pulling out the Amplifier."

I wince as I watch his bloody fingers crush the small plate, remembering how I did the same thing to myself two years ago. He yanks the rest of the implant out and tosses it aside, then tears off a piece of his sleeve to bandage up his open wound.

I exhale slowly. I feel like a huge burden has been lifted off of my shoulders. Miles turns to me and smiles. Then he quickly reaches behind my neck. I feel some pressure and then I black out.

Chapter 21

I'm brought back to consciousness by the sensation of being rocked back and forth. I slowly open my eyes and find myself on the floor of an empty van. My hands are tied behind my back and I have thick tape covering my mouth. I look up and see Miles in the driver's seat in front of me.

It looks like I've been kidnapped. It's just as well, I needed to get out of the prison anyway. Once everyone gets back to normal they'll realize what really happened, and there's no way I'd be able to talk my way out of all the evidence pointing to me. However, I don't appreciate being abducted like this. I understand that maybe Miles wants to get his revenge, but it's frustrating just how many times he's rendered me unconscious.

I scoot to the front of the van and wriggle up into the passenger's seat, which is difficult since I can't use my arms.

"I didn't give you permission to sit there," Miles remarks coldly. I just shrug my shoulders in reply.

"I still don't trust you, in case you were wondering why you're tied up and gagged," Miles explains. I tilt my head to the side. *Fair enough.*

"I'm taking you to the Dissenter base," he continues. "I figure they probably have a lot of questions they'll want to ask you."

That's good, I think. *At least he's not planning to throw me off a cliff somewhere.*

I stare out the window into the dusk. After a few moments I realize there are several vehicles behind us. I look over at Miles in alarm.

"They're with me," he assures me. "I released some of the prisoners who were Dissenters, including the Fioras."

I raise my eyebrows.

"Yes, Jacqueline and Brexlynn's parents," he confirms.

I look around at the van.

"We found these vehicles just outside the prison" he says, guessing my thoughts.

I let out a small laugh, which sounds muffled through the tape.

"Yeah, I guess it is funny that I know what you're thinking even though you can't talk."

I nod in agreement. He smiles at me, but then his face gets serious again. I can imagine what's going through his mind. He can't be friendly with me, I'm his captive. I'm the reason he spent months in jail being experimented on and conditioned with the Override.

We ride along in silence for a while. The sun is disappearing, but it's still fairly easy to see the vast desert landscape we're driving through. After some time Miles speaks again.

"I understand now how hard it must have been for you to resist killing me when we met on the air barge two years ago," he says softly. "I get how powerful the Override is now, so I can forgive you for that, at least."

I shift uncomfortably in the chair. Embedded in that statement are all the things he still holds against me. Like getting Amplified. Twice.

Suddenly Miles stops the van and gets out. The other vehicles pull up next to us. Miles opens my door and lifts me out. My body stiffens. In different circumstances it might be a nice gesture, but considering I'm being dragged around against my will I don't much appreciate the courtesy.

The other former prisoners have gotten out of their vehicles as well. There are seven of them. We appear to be in the middle of nowhere, and everyone just stands around. I guess we're waiting for something.

Minutes later I see headlights coming toward us. I look quizzically at Miles.

"Rescue protocol," he states. "We sent them a message through surveillance just outside of Compound U."

Two trucks approach. Blaine emerges from the first one and Felix jumps out of the second. *Felix can drive?* I think, wondering how the 10-year-old's short legs can even reach the pedals. I guess when you're a Dissenter spy you learn to do all sorts of things early. When Felix sees Miles he runs up and hugs him.

"I'm so glad you got out!" He exclaims. "Everyone's been so worried about you!" Felix glances over at me. "Oh hi, Mari!" He says casually, seemingly not caring that I'm tied up. I nod my head at him. Blaine comes over and slaps Miles on the back, then goes to greet the others. They pile into the beds of the two trucks, but Miles puts me in the passenger's seat of the truck Felix is driving. I don't know if he's doing it to be nice or because he's afraid I might try to jump out of the back, but either way I'm grateful.

We begin heading toward the Dissenter base and Felix starts chatting away.

"It must have been miserable at the prison, Mari. I was only there for a few hours to check it out, and it gave me the creeps," he remarks. "We're trying to ease the Community off of the Amplifiers, just like you suggested a few months ago at the meeting, but Roxy would never admit that it was your idea."

I smile. It's clear Roxy doesn't like me, and I don't agree with everything she does, but I'm glad she's implementing ideas that make sense.

"Blaine figured out a way to alter the Euphorics so that they break down the Amplifiers," he explains excitedly. "Then we released all the animals from the Preserve..."

"What?" I exclaim through the tape, so it sounds more like, "Mwaph?"

"Yeah," Felix responds, smiling. "This way, the Community will have to figure out how to make their own food instead of using the capsules."

So that's what the buffalo stampede through the East was about, I think. I'm all for the Community switching to eating real food, but I'm not sure setting all the animals free was a good idea.

Before I know it we're lowering down on the platform into the Dissenter base. All of Felix's talking must have made the time pass more quickly. I swallow hard. Felix has treated me the same as always, but I don't know how everyone else is going to feel about me showing up here. I did, after all, directly betray their leader and cause one of their own to be brutally imprisoned for the last several months. I guess I'll find out soon.

Even before everyone is out of the trucks the door to the entry chamber bursts open and a small crowd rushes forward to welcome Miles and the other rescued prisoners. I hang back as I watch Brexlynn and Jacqueline embrace their parents and a dozen others reach out to smother Miles. I wish my mom and Daniel were here, but I'm not sure if they'd actually be happy to see me.

Sabrina pushes through the group surrounding Miles and nearly attacks him with a hug.

"I missed you so much!" She sobs with so much emotion that even *I* blush. "How did you all escape?" She asks.

"It was all thanks to Mari, actually," Miles replies, glancing back at me. The room goes silent as all eyes turn to me. Sabrina looks like she wishes she could melt me with her stare, and several others are giving me less than friendly looks. Brexlynn gives me a small wave and a few appear to be sympathetic, but otherwise the reception is frigid.

Roxy steps forward. "Miles, would you help me take her to the shaft?" She asks solemnly. Miles takes a deep breath, clearly disappointed with my destination, but he takes my arm and follows Roxy down the hall. I don't know what "the shaft" is, but it sounds far worse than the regular holding cell I thought they were going to keep me in.

We wind through several hallways and passages until we reach the end of a dark corridor. Miles opens a short door which reveals a small compartment completely encased by walls of slick rock. I step in and notice a few tiny cracks for ventilation, but other than that it's a completely impenetrable room. Miles unties my hands, gives me one last unreadable look, then shuts the door and locks me in. With my hands now free I'm able to carefully remove the thick tape from my mouth. In complete blackness I curl up on the cold floor and attempt to go to sleep.

Chapter 22

"Felicia, you absolutely cannot see her without Roxy's permission."

"But I won't *see* her! I'm blind!"

The guard outside of the shaft does not appreciate my mom's joke.

"Okay, I'll go talk to Roxy," my mom concedes. I listen to her walk away on the other side of the door, glad that she at least wants to talk to me even if the guard didn't let her in.

I did sleep a little, but now my neck is extremely stiff. Despite my situation I'm actually feeling pretty optimistic. Alia came back from the North and Miles got out of prison. Two down, one to go. I don't know what the Dissenters are planning to do with me, but I'm hoping the fact that I helped Miles escape will sway their decision.

There are tiny points of light seeping through the ventilation cracks of the shaft. It's just enough to give a dim illumination to the small room. There's not much to see. I run my hands along all the walls, looking for any kind of opening, but it's all continuous, solid rock. I am completely trapped.

I jump as I hear something outside the door. I'm hoping my mother got permission to talk to me. The door opens. I squint at the light flooding in, struggling to make out who is entering. It's not my mother. It's someone much shorter and bulkier. The door closes and once my eyes adjust again I see my little brother holding a light stick and wearing the oddest suit I've ever seen.

"Daniel!" I exclaim. "What are you wearing?"

"It's flexible armor," he responds. "I had to wear it in order to come see you, so I'd be protected. But," he adds, shaking himself out of the bulky suit, "I really don't think you're going to hurt me."

I laugh and pull him toward me, hugging him so tightly that he starts to squirm.

"Ok, maybe I should have kept the armor on," he jokes, his voice muffled in my shoulder. I release him and we sit on the hard floor. There's barely enough room for us both to stretch our legs out.

"How have you been?" I ask him. "I see that they're letting you go on missions now," I say, remembering how he was with the Dissenters the day they blew up the Governor's mansion.

"Yeah, it's been great!" He tells me enthusiastically. "I almost got caught by a soldier last week when I was switching out some of the Euphorics pills, but I hid in a crate until she left."

"Wow, sounds exciting," I respond, trying not to imagine what would have happened if my brother had actually been discovered by the soldier.

"We're going to deliver some more Euphorics to the Community tomorrow too," Daniel continues. "We figured it'd be a good time since almost all of the Restrainers were sent to the East."

"Really?"

"Yeah, the Governor sent a whole convoy out there."

I sit forward, wondering why the Governor would send all the Restrainers out there when he'd already gotten all the information he wanted from us.

"Anyway," Daniel says a little awkwardly, "what's it like to be a Restrainer?" It's hard to see his face with just the light stick, but he seems a little strained.

"It's pretty lame, to be honest," I reply. "They all kind of hate me."

"But what's it like to have the enhanced Amplifier?" Daniel presses. "Have you done any really cool stuff?"

"Well, actually... " I stop when I notice something flashing on Daniel's shoulder. "What's that?" I ask, pointing to the flashing light.

"Um, it's... "

I look at it more closely. "Daniel, is that a microphone?" I say incredulously.

"Don't be angry, Mari!" He pleads. "That's the other thing I had to agree to do in order to see you!"

"I can't believe it! You're spying on me!" I groan, shaking my head in disappointment. I shouldn't be surprised. Daniel, who faked a stutter for years, would be the best candidate to subtly obtain information from me.

"Who asked you to do this?" I demand.

"Miles," he responds weakly.

I grab the microphone on Daniel's shoulder and hold it up to my mouth. "You can tell Miles that if he wants to know anything he should just come ask me himself!"

The door opens and I see Miles' large frame silhouetted against the light from the hallway.

"Well, thanks anyway Daniel," he says.

"Sure," Daniel replies sheepishly. He gives me one more apologetic look. "Sorry," he squeaks, then grabs the armor and scampers out of the shaft.

Miles sighs. He comes in, shutting the door behind him, and sits down on the floor next to me. I try to scoot away so that I'm not touching him, but it's impossible in the cramped space. He turns on a small electric lantern which lights up the shaft. I can now see the walls are made of limestone, the same that surround the cavernous lake. I glance over at Miles. He's cut his hair and he looks well rested. I make myself look away. Now is not the time to be distracted by how attractive he is.

"My own brother, Miles? Really?"

"I know," he confesses, "that was pretty underhanded."

I wait for him to interrogate me, but he says nothing. "So, how long are you going to keep me here?" I ask coldly.

Miles takes a while to answer. "They're going to put you on trial."

"For what?"

"For betraying us, for endangering me, and for using the Dissenters to secure yourself a position with the Restrainers."

"Is that what you think I did?"

"Unfortunately," Miles continues, ignoring my question, "with everything that's going on, we won't be able to start your trial until next week."

Next week? I've held up all right in this little room for a night, but spending several days in here might just make me go crazy. I'm not worried about the trial. If it comes down to it, I'll just tell them the truth. Although I might have a hard time proving it.

"There are actually quite a few people that are glad you're here," Miles announces, suddenly changing the subject.

"Like who?"

"Talina, for one."

"Really?"

"Well, I don't know that it's so much you as your transmitter, but since you've been here she's been using her Amplifier non stop. It's actually been pretty annoying."

I grin. My former head trainer and the only Dissenter who's Amplified told me once how much she missed being able to use it. I look over at Miles again. Just him being here makes the whole room warmer. I suddenly flush a little at the thought of how near he is.

"So why aren't you taking any precautions now?" I ask, genuinely wanting to know. "Yesterday you tied me up and silenced me. Aren't you afraid that I'm going to try to use my Amplifier against you?"

"I did that yesterday mainly for the benefit of the others," Miles responds. "I know that you would never physically hurt me."

I nod slowly, noting the designation. What he means is I don't need my Amplifier to hurt him emotionally.

We sit in silence for a few moments.

"Do you ever wonder what it would be like if there were no Amplifiers?" Miles asks unexpectedly.

"All the time," I admit.

"I just think that if there was no Amplification things would have been different between us."

I groan, feeling like we've had this conversation before. "No," I respond, "things would not be different between us, because you'd probably just get hung up on another one of my many flaws."

"Yeah? Like what?"

"I don't know, that my eyes are too big or something."

He laughs. "Mari, your eyes are perfect."

My pulse quickens. Luckily it's dim enough that Miles can't tell I'm blushing. I glance over and notice that he's staring at the floor.

"You really do love being Amplified, don't you?" He asks hopelessly.

I swallow hard. I should tell him the truth, but I can't. It's probably my stupid, stubborn pride. But I can at least tell him part of it.

"Miles," I say quietly, "I did this mostly for you."

"For me?" He replies, suddenly agitated. "Mari, it'd be better if you had never gotten Amplified in the first place, if you had never become a Restrainer!"

"Well, it happened, Miles!" I shout, frustrated with his obstinance. "I can't change that now! The only thing that can change is whether you accept me or not!"

"Why do you care if I accept you?"

"Because I love you Miles! I have always loved you!"

There it is. I said it. Each word hangs in the air. Miles stares at me, his eyes warm and his mouth slightly open. But then his expression hardens and I see the sadness seep back into his eyes. Looking at him now I can see just how much the months in prison and the Override experiments took out of him. There is doubt and bitterness where there used to be confidence and resilience.

"I can't trust you, Mari," he says shakily. "Your choices contradict your words."

He slowly gets up and starts to leave, then turns back, pulling a small bag out of his pocket.

"I brought this for you," he mutters, placing the bag in front of me. Then he takes his lantern and walks out, shutting the door and leaving me in darkness again.

I pull my knees up and rest my head on them. I'm being stupid. I should have told him everything. It's selfish to expect Miles to love me despite the decisions and allegiances he thinks I've made.

I pick up the bag Miles left and reach inside. There's a small bottle of water and three other small, wet objects. I smell them and know what they are immediately. Strawberries. My heart sinks. I've caused Miles so much pain, and yet he's still thoughtful enough to remember the first real food I ever ate. Hopefully after I finish everything I plan to do all of this will be worth it.

Chapter 23

I'm surprised when the door opens. I have no concept of time in this dark room, but I'm guessing it's the middle of the night. I'm even more surprised when I see it's Blaine. I don't think he's ever really liked me very much, so I don't know why he'd want to visit me. He doesn't come in, he just stands in the hallway and leaves the door open.

"How are you doing, Mari?" He asks.

"Fine, considering everything," I reply hesitantly. There's something weird about the way Blaine is standing, the way he keeps looking back down the hall. It makes me nervous.

"Miles told you we're putting you on trial, right?"

"Yes."

"Problem is, it's going to take a while for us to get around to it. Too long, in my opinion. So I figured I'd just take care of this now."

He's going to kill me! I think. *He doesn't want to waste everybody's time by going through a trial, so he's just going to get rid of me now!*

I shrink back into the corner as he takes a step forward.

"I've been watching you," he says, pulling something out from under his arm. I tense up. "I know what you're doing," he continues, "and I think it's brilliant."

Wait, what?

"I don't know exactly what your plan is, but I'm guessing it doesn't involve being imprisoned down here."

I exhale slowly. "What do you mean?"

"I'm letting you out, Mari, but you're going to have to be quick."

I get up slowly, still not completely convinced that he's not going to kill me.

"I'll need you to wear this," he explains, handing me a bundle of fabric which turns out to be a long jacket. "We put you in the shaft partly because it conceals the signal from your transmitter so well, but once you come out of here and especially when you get above ground you'll be completely visible on their radar, and I imagine they'll be looking for you. The collar on that jacket will cover up your Amplifier's signal, so make sure you keep it up. There's a vehicle in the entry chamber you can use to get out."

I stare at Blaine in disbelief as I put on the jacket.

"Thank you," I say simply.

"Get going," he responds impatiently, again looking nervously down the hall.

I take off running, moving through the dark hallways as quietly as I can. I make it to the entry chamber and expect to see a truck, but what I find instead is one of Blaine's modified monster tractors. It's going to be a fun night.

I hide the tractor in some abandoned buildings just outside of the city. It would be a shame for such a fine and exhilarating piece of equipment to be destroyed or stolen. I walk the remaining quarter mile to the outskirts of the city.

Blaine said he didn't know what my plan was. Unfortunately, neither do I. Because of my stunt at the prison I'm positive I'm in trouble with the Community, and the safest thing for me might just have been to stay locked up at the Dissenter base. But things seem to be progressing rapidly, so there really is no time to waste.

I creep around some buildings and come to a plaza. I gasp. My face is everywhere. On every building a screen with my face on it glows in the darkness. I step up to one to see what it says.

"Reward for the capture of the former Restrainer Marianna Quillen. Anyone involved in the seizure of this criminal will receive enhanced Amplification."

Great, I think, *now everyone is really motivated to catch me.* Nearly everybody in the Community would love to have increased abilities and be on the same level as the Restrainers.

I clearly won't be able to walk around in the daytime, so I better take advantage of the time I have right now. I make my way over to the new building, wanting to see if anything has changed. When I get there

I see there's a light on inside. I find one of the back doors open and I slip in.

Directly in front of me are stacks of empty crates. A piece of paper floats down next to my foot. I pick it up and move toward a light so I can read it. My mouth goes dry. On the paper are the designs from General Remington's Hybrid Experiment. I peer through the slats in the crates and see that the immense room that was once empty is now full of operating tables and robot parts. From the ceiling hang various instruments. It looks exactly like the room we saw in the North, only much bigger.

I am shocked. I knew the Governor was unstable, but I never imagined he was demented enough to carry on with General Remington's work; to turn everyone in the Community into immortal, unfeeling, demi-robots. This is disastrous. I don't care how reliant people may have become on their Amplifiers and the Override, I'm positive that most of them would be resistant to this idea.

I have to tell someone, but who? Everyone here is trying to capture me and most of the Dissenters think I'm a traitor. I doubt anyone would believe me. My best bet right now is Adrian, but I'm not even sure he'll be on my side.

When I get outside again the sun is just starting to come up. I fold up the paper with the designs and walk quickly over to Adrian's apartment building. There are a few people out, but they're either too busy or too tired to pay much attention to me.

I knock softly on Adrian's door and a few moments later it opens just a crack. Adrian peers out at me, his eyes growing wide. For a minute I don't think he's going to let me in, but then he flings the door open and pulls me quickly inside.

"Mari," he hisses, "what's going on? What did you do to become a criminal?"

"I released Miles Paxton from prison."

"What? Prisoner 568?"

"Yes, Miles Paxton."

"Why?"

"Because he's not the bad guy."

"But he's a Dissenter! Those people are barbarians!"

I blow my hair out of my face. It's time to tell him the truth.

"Our mother is one of those people. So is Daniel."

Adrian's jaw drops. "What are you saying, Mari? Have you gone crazy? Mom and Daniel are dead."

"No, they're not," I state firmly. "They're with the Dissenters. Mom has been a Dissenter since before we were born. Her and dad were some of the first. Think about it. The way we were raised? The games?"

Adrian doesn't say anything, but he nods his head slowly.

"Mom realized the Restrainers were starting to suspect her," I explain, "so she had the house blown up to make it look like her and Daniel had died."

"So they're alive?" Adrian murmurs, a glimmer of hope creeping into his eyes.

"Yes," I affirm. "And by the way, Daniel's stutter is fake."

"What?" Adrian roars.

"That's about how I reacted when I found out," I say.

"Where are they?" Adrian asks. "Can I see them?"

"Another time," I answer. "Right now, I need your help."

"With what?"

"The Governor is planning to perform an operation on everyone."

"Are you sure?"

"Yes. Look at this," I say, handing him the paper I found. He studies it for a moment.

"That doesn't seem so bad," he muses. "We would live forever."

"It's very bad!" I counter. "This is what they were doing in the North and they all died because of it!"

"You went to the North?"

"Yes," I respond. "They had all undergone this operation, but they couldn't let themselves feel anything too strongly because it would kill them. They could barely have emotions!"

"What do you mean?"

"If they got too angry or afraid or passionate, it would destroy their systems. Adrian, if you have this operation, you won't be able to feel any grief or joy. You won't be able to do anything with all of your girlfriends," I finish awkwardly.

"That would be horrible," he says, frowning, finally getting the point. "What do you want me to do?"

"Remove your Amplifier."

Adrian's face goes pale. "Mari, you can't ask me to do that."

"That's the only way you can avoid having this operation," I tell him. "I'm positive the Governor will use the Override to do this to everybody."

"But I'm nothing without my Amplifier."

"Adrian," I yell, "listen to yourself! You are so much more than a piece of technology in your neck!"

"The Amplifiers are the best thing that ever happened to us!" Adrian yells back.

"No, they're not! They've made us lazy and dependent and selfish! Think about it Adrian! What makes you more happy? Having your Amplifier or having people you love? Commanding your Amplifier to do something or doing it yourself? When was the last time you were really happy?"

Adrian sits down and rubs his forehead. "I don't know, Mari, this is a lot to take in."

"Well, this is your opportunity to take responsibility for yourself," I say, turning to go. "You can either live a full life now, or a fraction of one forever." I leave Adrian with his head in his hands. I can't waste any more time trying to convince him. He has to make his own choice.

Chapter 24

Alia and Liam are speechless as they stare at me. I've just finished telling them what I saw at the new building and the Hybrid designs. Juro looks up at Alia from his place on her lap, frowning at her scared expression.

"Maybe they're using those designs for something else, like building new machinery or something," Liam says hopefully.

"Do you really think the Governor's going to go to all this trouble for new machinery?" I respond.

"No, this is the perfect way for him to control everybody," Alia admits fearfully. "What can we do?"

"We can try to destroy all the instruments and surgical equipment on the ceiling," I suggest.

"Yeah, but there are only three of us," Liam interjects. "We'll only get so far before they stop us."

"We have to let more people know," I state. "If we tell everyone the Governor's plan, I'm sure we can get more people to resist."

"Only Liam and I can do that," Alia says. "There's no way you'd be able to be out in the open talking to people, Mari. I still can't believe you made it all the way over here without getting caught."

After I left Adrian's apartment, I slipped into the hospital to grab some bandages. I covered half of my face with them and walked over to the soldier's barracks on the east side of the Mall-cruiser station. Apparently, no one suspected anything.

"Luck, I guess," I finally reply.

Suddenly, the door to the small room is kicked open and four surly looking men rush in and grab me. Looks like my luck has just run out.

"This is definitely her," one of them growls.

I struggle to free myself and hear Alia and Liam command themselves.

"Liam, kick the men unconscious."

"Alia, get Mari out of their reach."

But before their commands can take effect, all four of the men calmly release me and lay down on the floor. At first I'm confused, but then I recognize the action as another command to lie still from the Override. I'm suddenly nauseous. I know now why those in the Override Program have been given this command so often; to prepare for the operation.

"Guys, it's happening now," I shout, turning around to face the others, but I only see Liam standing there. I look down and see Alia lying motionless on the floor, her eyes full of fear. Juro crouches next to her face, whimpering.

"The Governor told her the only way she could keep Juro was to sign on with the Override Program," Liam explains nervously.

I peer down at my friend. Her terrified eyes flit from Liam, to Juro, to me. I can't just let her be carried off and turned into a Hybrid.

"Alia," I say quickly, "if you want me to remove your Amplifier, look at the door."

Alia only hesitates a moment before she very deliberately looks toward the door. Liam looks apprehensive as he turns her on her side and fishes a small knife out of his pocket. I take the knife and carefully cut open the skin behind her ear, digging down until I find the small base of the Amplifier. I crush it and she spasms. Liam has to hold her still while I pull out the wires.

"Dang it, Mari! Why didn't you tell me it was going to hurt so much?" She grumbles through a grim smile. I use the bandages I took from the hospital to cover her open wound. She gets up shakily and kisses Liam, then reaches down to take Juro in her arms.

"We need to find a safe place for him," I state, gesturing to the little boy.

"One of the sleeping pods on the Mall-cruiser?" Liam suggests.

Alia looks doubtful, but no one else has any better suggestions, so we head over to the station.

Everything is eerily quiet. We pass dozens of people lying on the ground and their eyes light up with recognition when they see me, but there's nothing they can do.

Juro protests a bit about being left in a sleeping pod, but once Alia finds some Adhesives for him to watch he calms down. Back outside the Mall-cruiser, we try to figure out our best course of action.

"Maybe we should just take out all of their Amplifiers," Alia proposes, looking out at everyone on the ground.

"That would take way too long," I remark. "Plus, some of them might actually want to become Hybrids. We can't just make that decision for them."

"What's a Hybrid?" Says a voice below us. I look down at our feet and see a girl propped up on her elbows. Liam yelps and jumps back.

"Are you okay?" I ask.

"Yeah. I'm a little uncomfortable, but otherwise, I'm fine," she answers casually.

"Are you on the Override Program?"
"Yes, but my Amplifier has been faulty ever since I took that tainted Euphorics pill. So now only half of my body obeys the Override commands," she explains, pointing at her lifeless legs.

I scan the bodies strewn on the ground and every once in a while I notice a bit of movement; a head turning or a leg twitching. I want to ask the girl more about her situation, but all at once I hear loud rumbling coming from behind the Mall-cruiser. We turn around and see a dozen massive vehicles coming over the ridge.

We run into the Mall-cruiser and watch the approaching vehicles through a small window.

They stop a few feet away from the compartment we're in, so we have a clear view of them. About a hundred Restrainers emerge from the vehicles, each carrying a large sack. Clint is one of the last to appear, and I hear him instruct the other Restrainers.

"Make sure you give a Euphorics pill to everyone, even if they're still moving."

The Restrainers move forward, stopping whenever they come to a body to shove a Euphorics pill in their mouth.

I'm wondering what the purpose of this procedure is when I remember something Adrian said about the Euphorics: *"You could bash my knees in with a metal beam right now and I wouldn't feel a thing!"* I think they might be administering the Euphorics so people don't feel anything during the operation, which actually seems pretty humane. Of course, they could also be ensuring that everyone is completely useless in case anything goes wrong with the Override.

When the last wave of Restrainers has disappeared into the city, we creep back out of the Mall-cruiser.

"If everyone is lying still, who's going to get all of these people to the new operation building?" Liam asks. "The Restrainers couldn't possibly handle that themselves."

In answer to his question, the vehicles behind us start creaking. The sides of the transports burst open and reveal thousands of familiar entities. They pour out of the vehicles, walking with jerky, robot-like movements, their cold, beautiful faces devoid of expression.

My stomach churns. The Governor has created a Hybrid army with all of the dead citizens of the East.

Chapter 25

I watch in horror as the gorgeous zombies methodically stoop down to pick people up and carry them in the direction of the operation building. Suddenly, one of them approaches us and its hand turns into a gun.

"Mari, disarm the robot."
I bring my leg up and kick the robot's gun, which causes its entire arm to detach, exposing a mess of metal and wires at its shoulder. Undeterred, it continues to advance, swiping at our heads with its other arm.

"Alia, decapitate the machine." Alia waits expectantly, but nothing happens.
"Oh yeah, I don't have an Amplifier," she laughs. She lashes her arm across the robot's neck, making its head pop off.

"Did you see that guys?" She exclaims. "I did that by myself!"

But we don't have time to celebrate. We've taken down one, but several others are coming for us.

"What do we do?" Liam shouts. "We can't take on all of them!"

"We could try pretending we're on the Override," I respond. "It might not work, but I think it's our best option."

"What will we do when we get to the operation building?" Alia spouts frantically, eyeing three of the robots starting to close in.

"No idea," I answer truthfully. "Hopefully one of us will think of something by then."

We all collapse to the ground and lie still just as the robots are beginning to look menacing. They come near us and hesitate. I don't know if there's someone on the other end directing all these machines or if they were just programmed to do certain things in different situations. I hold my breath as the robots stand there, unmoving. Finally, their automatic arms reach down and lift us up. I try to stay as limp as possible as they carry us toward the new building.

Once we're brought inside, we're all laid on tables next to other Overriden citizens. I look around as much as I can without moving my head. I spot Joby close by, his eyes glazed over from the effects of the Euphorics pill. A robot stands motionless next to each operating table. After a few minutes, the intimidating array of instruments on the ceiling begin to lower. Most of the instruments are large and sharp. I figure I can grab a couple of them to take out all the robots nearby and hope that Alia and Liam follow my lead.

When the racks of instruments have almost reached us, a sudden scuffle breaks out in the middle of the room. I risk being found out and sit up to see what's going on. It's Adrian. My hearts soars as I watch him stand on top of his operating table, kicking off the heads of every robot that approaches him. I can see the blood marks on his neck from where he removed his Amplifier. I guess after all this time we still think alike.

Liam, Alia and I join in the growing chaos, using the instruments or kicks and punches to incapacitate the beautiful machines surrounding us. We make a small dent in the robot ranks, but we're nowhere near stopping this demonic plan. Someone has to be controlling all of this. In between knocking out robots, I look around for some Restrainers, but I find them all in a far corner lying on tables waiting to have the operation done themselves.

Then I see him. On the far wall near the ceiling is a small window where Clint's face peers anxiously out. He must be the one orchestrating everything in here.

"Hey, I'm going to go check something out," I yell to Alia.

"All right," she replies shakily as she twists off a robot's arm.

I grab onto the nearest instrument hanging from the ceiling and propel myself in the direction of the window, swinging from one instrument to the next until I reach the wall and crash feet first through the glass. I stand up and face Clint. To my surprise, he's smiling.

"I'm so glad you're here, Mari," he admits, reaching into a box next to him. "Here, tie me up with these bandages."

"Are you serious?" I ask, thoroughly confused.

"Absolutely," Clint responds. "Look, I knew something was going to go wrong with all this and frankly, I think this whole Hybrid thing is a bad idea. I don't want to go through with this, and I'd much rather have the Governor be angry at you than at me for thwarting his crazy plan."

I roll my eyes and tie Clint's hands behind the chair he's sitting in.

"Press the reset button after you're done," he instructs, nodding at a large button on the panel in front of him. I tie his legs to the chair and wrap a bandage around his mouth. I turn and push the reset button and watch the racks of instruments return to the ceiling, but the robots are still engaged with Adrian, Liam, and Alia, as well as a few others with faulty Amplifiers that are deliriously swinging their arms and legs at the machines. I look back at Clint. He just shrugs his shoulders. I growl in frustration and hastily find the stairs that will lead me back into the massive room.

I see Alia, Liam, and Adrian are still fending off attacking robots, but they're exhausted, and a lot of people lying on the tables are getting injured.
"Maybe if we leave the building, they'll follow us out," I suggest. Alia and Liam agree and I call over to Adrian to come with us. We run toward the doors and discover that the robots are much faster than we had expected. We're nearly outside when something small crashes through the window nearest to us and lands at our feet.

"Bomb!" Liam yells, grabbing Alia and running for cover. But the small black device doesn't explode.

Instead, all the lights shut off and the robots appear to shut down. I see their arms hanging limply at their sides in the dim light that filters through the window. Everyone on the operating tables sits up and looks around, laughing or screaming in their Euphoric hysteria.

We walk outside and I see the most wonderful thing I could have imagined. Four trucks of Dissenters are parked in front of the building, with Miles on top of the closest one. I smile instinctively at him, the way I always used to when we were kids.

Alia and Liam look terrified as the Dissenters start jumping out of the trucks.

"They won't hurt us," I assure them, but their expressions don't change. Blaine emerges from a truck and runs up to us.

"So it worked?" He asks.

"Yeah," I reply. "What was that?"

"An electromagnetic pulse was contained in that little device," he explains proudly. "We shot it out of our range so we wouldn't lose power in the trucks, but it should have wiped out all of the electricity in the city."

I'm startled by a small figure that darts past me and embraces Adrian.

"Daniel!" Adrian exclaims, lifting his little brother off the ground. Daniel then grabs his hand and takes him over to my mother, who's standing quietly at the back of the group of Dissenters.

"Mari."

I turn around and find myself face to face with Miles.

"Look," I begin, trying to avoid his eyes, "I'm sorry that I escaped, but the thing is-"

"Mari, I love you," he interrupts suddenly, fervently. "I don't care that you're Amplified. I've tried to get you out of my mind, but I can't because I don't want to. Mari, you're my world."

Then he takes my face in his strong hands and kisses me. All I feel is fire. Fire behind my eyelids and spreading through my body to my toes and fingertips. I could burn like this forever, but the moment is shattered by the sounds of gunshots and screaming.

We break apart and I try to make sense of what's going on.

"Someone has reversed the EMP!" I hear Blaine yelling. Robots are surrounding the Dissenters, but the Dissenters are holding them off pretty well with their guns. I focus on a cluster of Dissenters and see something that makes my body go cold.

Adrian has been shot.

Chapter 26

I run through the Dissenters to get to my brother. He's on the ground, surrounded by his own blood. I kneel down beside him.

"What happened?" I ask frantically.

"The robot came from behind and shot at mom, but Adrian jumped in front of her," Daniel chokes out. My mom is laying next to him and sobbing. I take Adrian's hand.

"I'm so sorry," I cry, "this is all my fault. You would have been safe in there if you hadn't taken out your Amplifier."

"No, Mari, you were right," he says softly. "The times when I was acting for myself, that's when I've been the most happy. This past hour has been a blast," he adds, smiling weakly. "I'd rather die like this than live forever as a slave." His eyes flutter and he tightens his grip on my hand. "I love you guys," he whispers. Then his eyes roll back and he exhales one last time.

I feel a part of me slip away. Tears are streaming down my face and I want to stay here and cry with my family, but there's a battle raging around us. I look up and see an air barge taking off about 200 feet beyond the hospital. I know instinctively that the Governor is on it. I know he reversed the EMP. I know he's responsible for the death of my brother. It's time to carry out the last part of my plan.

I get up and start running toward the air barge.

"Where are you going?" Miles asks, catching me by the arm.

Looking into his honey-colored eyes I momentarily forget everything, but then a decapitated robot staggers in between us and brings me back to my sense of purpose.

"Do you have any of those micro parachutes Blaine developed?" I ask him.

"I have one."

"Great, come with me."

I tell him the Governor is on the air barge as we run to it, but other than that I really don't have a plan. He doesn't seem to mind.

The air barge is already 60 feet in the air, and we immediately start climbing the cables up to it. I climb slightly faster than Miles and just barely beat him to the top. I can't help but notice that he's a little disgruntled about it.

"If you didn't have an Amplifier..." he grumbles. I smile to myself.

I look across the expansive deck of the structure and realize this is the training barge. I see the buildings that house the classrooms and dorms, the Coliseum, the Nutrition Hall, the recording room on the far side. *The recording room!* Suddenly, I have a plan.

"This way," I tell Miles. "I need you to help me make an Adhesive."

"Mari, is this really the time?"
"Absolutely."

———-

We peer out from behind a wall in the urban obstacle course. I'm guessing the Governor is here somewhere in the Coliseum. I have the Adhesive we just made in the pocket of my jacket, I'm just hoping I'll be able to use it.

"My best guess is that he's in there," Miles whispers, pointing across the Coliseum to the electrocution room.

I swallow hard as I recall the demonic jungle of electrically charged cables that are impossible to get through unless the electricity is turned off. We keep close to the walls as we cross to the room. We approach the entrance and I can hear the buzz of the live wires.

"We should turn off the electricity," I say quietly.

"If we do, Governor Plenaris will know that we're here," Miles responds.

"He probably already does."

Miles nods in agreement, and I go to the side of the entrance to turn off the switch.

"I'll go first," Miles announces.

"Why not go together?"

"Because if it's deadly in there, at least one of us will still be alive."

I hate his logic, but I let him go in. He disappears into the mess of cables. After a few long moments I hear Miles yelping and wires snapping. I rush forward to try and find him in the maze, but before I've even taken three steps the cables start to lift up into the ceiling, revealing the Governor and a large array of screens and controls where Override machines used to be hidden.

"Miss Quillen," Governor Plenaris remarks, spreading his arms in an odd gesture of welcome, "I'm so glad you've found me. And how wonderful you brought your *special* friend with you," he adds, glancing up at the cables. I see Miles hopelessly tangled in the wires. He's facing downward and he can barely move his limbs.

"I'll admit, Miss Quillen, I've been a bit lazy lately, letting you slip under my radar while I've been preoccupied with bigger plans."

I look at the screens behind him and see the battle going on below. The Dissenters are doing a lot of damage, but half of the robots have returned to the operation building where people are back on the tables, the instruments again lowered and ready to assist with the dreaded surgery.

"Yes, I always had complete command of the Hybrid operation," he states, noticing my fallen expression. "I had only hoped Clint would take care of it so I didn't have so much on my hands today."

"Why?" I spit out. "Why was this necessary? Weren't you satisfied with the level of control you had?"

"Of course not," he replies. "I'm never satisfied. It was all right using the Override for a while," he explains, "but when left to themselves, people would make so many mistakes. They'd choose the wrong thing, they'd waste this incredible potential given to them. When General Remington showed up with his plan to make us all Hybrids, I realized this was the next natural step for the perfection of our Community."

"If it was so natural, why didn't you tell anyone about this?" I ask, feverishly rubbing the tip of my shortened finger.

"Miss Quillen, people don't know what they want. I couldn't trust them to make the right decision. Once they get used to it, they'll realize that this is ideal. Their robotic parts fused with their Amplifiers will ensure them immortality. They'll be completely taken care of for the rest of their very long lives."

"Why involve the East?" I nearly shout. "What was the point of disturbing all of those corpses by filling them with machinery?"

"We put them to good use," the Governor scoffs. "Plus, I wanted to test the Hybrid designs on them first to ensure all would go well with live subjects."

It's incredible, I think. *He speaks about it all so calmly, and yet what he's saying is completely ludicrous.*

"What about you?" I taunt. "Why aren't you being subjected to this Hybrid operation?"

"Well, Marianna, my eternity is far more exciting than just robotic parts. Your handler, Clint, was kind enough to bring back the last of the East's preservative. Diluted, the formula won't kill me, but will conserve me as I am forever, provided that my organs continue to be replenished from generous donors. This is where Mr. Paxton comes in, actually."

"What?" I wheeze, feeling like someone has punched me in the stomach.

"He'll be the first donor," Governor Plenaris says simply. "You see, all that time in prison he wasn't being trained to fight, but rather to comply. After a little more discipline, he'll be ready to give me parts of his brain, his lungs, and of course, his eyes."

I hear Miles coughing and choking above me, probably trying to keep himself from vomiting like I am. This surpasses all of my nightmares. I never imagined that the Governor, with all of his sadistic plans for power and perfection, would be capable of something like this.

"So, Miss Quillen," the Governor announces, "you have been... *entertaining*, but as always, it seems that you're standing in the way of my goals. I'm going to kill you, but first I'll need you to re-Amplify your friend here, and then I can get back to immortalizing the Community."

He pushes a few buttons and the section of cables that Miles is caught in lowers to the ground. Then the Governor slides a tray over to me with an Amplifier and several small knives on it. He looks straight at me and activates his personal Override, the band on his wrist that allows him to command another person with only his thoughts.

"Mari, Amplify Miles Paxton."

I shiver at his voice in my head, but otherwise, I don't move.

"I thought Restrainers were exempt from the Override," I hiss.

"Generally, they are," the Governor responds, only slightly unnerved that his command has no effect on me, "but based on your behavior over the last few days, you have most certainly been stripped of your position."

He presses the band on his wrist again.

"Marianna, Amplify Miles Paxton."

This time I smile at his perplexed expression.

"I knew I couldn't trust you with the Override," I explain calmly, "so I decided to take some extra precautions."

The Governor frantically turns around and brings up old surveillance footage on one of the screens, searching until he finds the day I received my second Amplifier. He watches the exchange between me and the technician as she programs the device in my head.

"Full name?"

"Marianna Quillen."

"And the name you will use to direct your Amplifier?"

"Clarence."

The Governor turns around and stares at me. All the hard work I did, all the times I pretended, all of the times I was despised by the Dissenters and my family and Miles; it was all worth it to see this look of terror on the Governor's face. He can't command me through his personal Override without also commanding himself, and if we both tried to implant Miles, we would risk messing it up or killing him.

Before the Governor can figure out a way around this, I lunge at him. His hand flies off of his Override band and for the first time I hear him actually give himself a command.

"Clarence, kill her by any means necessary."

I stumble back as I witness the most extreme case of inequality I've ever seen. The Governor jumps and literally flies at my face. It's clear that his Amplifier is not only enhanced, it's super human.

I dive out of the way, but he changes direction in mid air and comes after me. I sprint to the wall and run up it to flip over, hoping he'll pursue me so fast that he slams into the wall. He does pursue me, but instead of crashing into the wall he kicks off of it and sprints faster than I can process over to the wall of weapons. He grabs a knife and hurls it at me from 300 feet away with deadly precision. I move just in time and it sticks in the wall where my head used to be. He pulls off a gun and fires it at me. I shield myself with the heavy tray that had the

Amplifier on it and manage to block the bullet, but the force of it knocks me to the ground.

He leaps, flips, and spins wildly through the air. Within fractions of a second he's on top of me, his hands around my neck and his eyes full of madness. I choke as I try to pry his fingers away, but his grip is too strong. I start to black out from the pain and loss of air. *Maybe I should just give up,* I think in my near delirium. *Dying would be really easy. I wouldn't have to resist anymore.* But then I look over and catch a glimpse of Miles and realize I have so much worth living for.

With strength I didn't know I had, I kick him in the groin and flip him off of me. Before he can retaliate, I whip the Adhesive out of my pocket and slap it onto his temple, then reach down and press the personal Override band on his wrist.

His eyes become vacant as the Adhesive takes over his optical and auditory systems, transporting him to the recording room where Miles is giving him a message. I made Miles say it three times over just to be safe.

"Clarence, command the robots to gather two miles south of the Mall-cruiser station, then turn off the air turbines and crash this air barge on top of them."

The Governor's eyes fill with crazed anger, but he stands and walks to the controls, directing the robots away from the operation building. He's bound by the command Miles indirectly spoke into his head through his personal Override. I wait until the Governor heads over to shut off the turbines to help Miles out of the cables.

It takes a little longer than I'd hoped to get Miles untangled, and for some reason he can't stop smiling at me. We're only halfway out of the Coliseum when I feel the floor jerk downwards from the turbines being turned off. We move as fast as we can, but it's hard to keep our feet on the floor as the barge picks up speed in its descent. We're practically airborne by the time we get out the door, and Miles struggles to pull me close to him and activate the micro parachute.

The parachute automatically deploys just seconds after Miles puts it on, proving what a close call it was. We float safely through the air as the massive barge speeds downward and crashes spectacularly into the ground, sending up stray particles of matter in the air. I'm holding on to Miles tightly, but I twist around to see the wreckage of the training barge.

We land just outside of the crash site. There are some electrical fires smoldering in what's left of the barge and I can see some arms and legs of the smashed robots sticking out of the rubble. It'd be morbid if they hadn't already been dead.

"I can't believe you, Mari," Miles laughs as he puts away the micro parachute. "You were Amplified all this time and you never used it! You lied to me!"

His smile is enough to make me melt, but I hold my ground.

"Not necessarily," I reply. "You never directly asked me about it."

"You are incredible, Mari," he says as he wraps his arms around me.

He kisses me and I'm filled with that fire again, but this time it's tinged with sadness from the loss of my brother. I realize that Miles won't be able to take the pain away, but he can soften it.

"Kissing me twice in one day?" I tease him as I pull away. "Miles, I'm shocked! Where's all your self control?"

His eyes fill with amusement.

"When you spend most of your life resisting," he says, smiling, "it makes the moments you give in that much more significant."

I roll my eyes as he pulls me in again, but I have to admit it's true.

Chapter 27

We buried Adrian next to my father. I look at his fresh gravestone, a modest cement slab that looks almost exactly like the one on my father's grave. It's interesting because my dad and Adrian were so different, but they both died with purpose. Wherever they are, I hope they're having a good time together.

The Governor ended up surviving the crash. I figured he would. He got out with a parachute or something before impact, but he broke his leg. That's probably how Roxy was able to catch him. The Dissenters headed over to the destroyed air barge after they saw it fall and on the way ran into the hobbling Governor. I don't know exactly how Roxy overtook him, but I would have loved to see that fight. She took out his Amplifier and she's going to put him on trial. It's not looking too good for him, especially since mostly everyone was outraged when they found out about the Hybrid plan.

The Dissenters have been welcomed back into the Community. I guess everyone is grateful that they helped hold off the operation. Now the Community is considering getting rid of the Amplifiers altogether, or at least limiting their capacities.

Miles and I decided we wanted to try to find the West. With the North's airship, I'm pretty confident we'll be able to figure out where they are before running out of supplies. At first we thought we would just take a small group with us, but once word spread that we'd be going more and more people became interested. There will be about 20 of us altogether, including my mom and Daniel, Alia, Liam, and Juro, Clint, Brice, Joby, Cassidy, Tristan (probably because he didn't want to get left behind), Blaine, Felix, and all of the Fioras. And lately, Joby and Brexlynn have been spending a lot of time together despite the strong objections from Brexlynn's parents. It's going be a fun trip.

    I look back at the gravestones of my deceased family members. We're leaving for the West today, and I wanted to come here one more time before we go just in case we never come back. I say my last goodbyes and start running back to the city. I almost trip as I try to untangle the wires of my ancient music device. I think about what Adrian would say if he could see me right now, and I smile. He would definitely make fun of me.

Printed in Great Britain
by Amazon